The Boundaries of My Heart

by
Grace True

First paperback edition April 2022

Book design by Publishing Push

ISBNs
Paperback: 978-1-80227-454-7
eBook: 978-1-80227-455-4

Dedication

I give thanks
to the
Lord God Almighty
who is my
Loving Father and Saviour.

And I give thanks to the Lord God
for my beautiful, amazing angels, Lawrence and Ophelia,
who fill my life with love, joy and many blessings.

Psalm 37:4-5

Delight yourself in the Lord,
and he will give you the desires of your heart.
Commit your way to the Lord; trust in him, and he will act.

I pray that you will be blessed
and will continue to be filled more and more with His Spirit
as you grow closer to the Lord.

Contents

Chapter 1

Memories

It was 5 pm and Sarah had just got home and parked her car on the driveway. As she closed the door of the car, she heard her neighbour's voice.

"Hello, Sarah. How was your day?"

"Hello, Jane. It was fine, thank you."

She had so many things in her hands, lots of files from work and bags of shopping, and Mrs. Marshall was still talking.

How could she carry them inside? For sure, she was not in the mood to go back and forth a few times. She managed slowly, and yes, Jane was still talking.

"Would you like me to help you, Sarah?"

"No, I am fine, thank you, Jane."

Mrs. Marshall was a lovely lady, a widow who had moved next door to Sarah a few years ago. She was full of kindness and always there for all her neighbours, but for some reason, she had become very fond of Sarah. She had never had children of her own and had only a sister and a few relatives living in the west of the country. She loved visiting them a few times a year, but her life was church and serving and Sarah.

John 3:16
For God so loved the world that he gave his only Son, that whoever believes in him should not perish but have eternal life.

1

After the death of Sarah's parents, she had taken her under her wing. She visited her and spoke to her; she was there all the time.

And if you're wondering whether Sarah was raised in the church – oh, no! The church was a definite no-no. You had to be very well-behaved to go to church. That was what she was told. Do this and do that. She felt she needed to be a saint just to enter a church. Church for her just brought back memories and reminded her of her past mistakes and sins. She had felt really bad when she used to go to church in her youth.

But Jane told her that God accepts us as we are and loves us as we are. Yes, you are loved and accepted, and in His grace, the Lord can help you and change you. That was new to Sarah and a bit confusing. It made her curious to know a bit more about God. She did need love and acceptance, and she had a heart full of memories.

Her parents, Andrew and Mary, two lonely, broken hearts, had met in their late 40s, so she was the only one born in the family. But let's not forget her stepbrothers, Mike and Joe, the two sons of her father from his first marriage. They were quite a challenge for her. It would be more truthful to say that they never liked her and were always mean to her. She was the other child of their father – not family or the other part of the family.

They were quite a lot older than her but always teased her and embarrassed her. She could still remember the family meetings. Her step-brothers would come over for dinner and take over the evening. They would brag about how good they were and how wonderful their jobs were and what good positions they had. Nobody asked her about her life, her job or even how she was. She just sat quietly at the corner of the table.

She did it for her parents. And she did it for years. It started when she was a little kid, and things got worse over the years. For her, quietness was good, and she learned to appreciate it. She learned to just close her heart, and in an instant, the evening was gone. She was invisible in a way. It used to hurt her, but she came to consider it a blessing. She did not want to be involved in conversations in which anything she said would be ignored or might be used to hurt her.

When her parents passed away, her stepbrothers told her they did not want anything more to do with her, and Jane was the only one who wanted to see her. It did not really bother her, as she had a successful career and lots of friends at work (if you could call them friends).

As she entered the house, she looked around. Nothing had changed. The same little dining table and the same four old chairs. The flowers in the vase had been wilted for days, and she'd forgotten to throw them away. She did not care much for the house; it carried too much hurt and too many memories.

To break the silence, she turned on the little TV in the kitchen and started unpacking. Wearily, she took things out one by one and put them on the dining table.

In front of her was a picture of her late parents. The TV news was on, and she saw a few lines written on the screen: *Tragic accident, no survivors.*

Her mind wrestled with memories, but she could not cry. She could not remember how many tears she had shed. Her soul was dry, with no hope. The accident had happened a few years ago, but she still felt the same.

She re-lived the moment when a man had knocked at their door and broken the news that her parents were no more. Ever since, she had tried to cope with it. How could she sell the house? It held so many memories! She was stuck and did not know what to do, but she really wanted to move on.

She was moving in circles, wrestling with the same thoughts over and over again. Home was not a place she wanted to be; it was not her home any longer. Maybe it had never been her home; it was just her parents' home.

Work, then home, and Mrs. Marshall, that was her life – and yes, church. Let's not forget she'd started to go to church. Incredible! She hadn't done anything new for years.

She, Sarah Grant, going to church? If you had told her that a few years ago, she would have laughed. Oh, Mrs. Marshall, what a lovely lady. She had her own way, and the Lord worked miracles through her.

The only one who kept coming was Mrs. Marshall. All her relatives left. Well, they were in it for the money, and they did get some, but Sarah got the house. Once they got their inheritance, they all disappeared without a word. Sarah was heartbroken that with all her family, she was alone.

It took her some time to deal with the pain, but she got better at it over the years. Accepting how things were was the first step she could take. She knew she needed support, not counselling, to help her to get up and go again. Move in any direction, anywhere.

"Don't worry, dear. Don't worry; things will get better. You will see: God will help you. Don't worry. God loves you," Jane kept saying.

But so far, nothing had changed. Same house, same job, stuck in the same day-to-day routine. When would it change? And how?

Her friends from the office made fun of her sometimes. She withdrew totally from the world, and each time they asked her to join them when they were going out, she would find an excuse. By now they had got it and stopped asking her; she was left in her bubble, forgotten. She would occasionally go to lunch with a friend or two, but never to parties, and without knowing, ended up rather like her parents, isolated and afraid.

The news was over, and a film had started. As she stood up, she decided to go straight to bed and left the kitchen full of shopping. Anyway, tomorrow was Saturday. Jane would be there to help her.

Jane Marshall had dedicated herself to looking after Sarah. She ended up even having a key to her house, so Sarah never knew when she would appear. Maybe she was the reason Sarah kept going, as Jane kept reminding her to keep going.

The bed was cold, and she closed her eyes. It felt so lonely.

She tried to pray; as Jane would say, "Talk to the Lord; he is here." Talk about what? That was a good question. There was so much to say and talk about, but did it really matter?

She could only say, "When are you going to help me, Lord? I am totally stuck, and I want to move on, to move somewhere, anywhere."

The night passed quickly and it was morning again.

There was a knock at the door and Sarah looked at her clock. It was already 8.30.

"I'm here, Sarah. Are you awake?"

Oh, no! She never lets me have a lie-in, thought Sarah, *and today is Saturday.* Jane never wanted to lie in – she was a morning person. Sarah turned over and huddled under the bed covers. *Five more minutes, just five more. My house is a mess, and I'm not in the mood for anything today.*

Jane called again from downstairs, so she jumped out of bed. She slowly put on her bathrobe and sat by the bed, looking into a void.

Another day, another Saturday.

Jane Marshall, with her beautiful white hair and lovely hazel eyes, came and hugged her. She always hugged her, and Sarah was not often in the mood for hugs. Her parents had never hugged her, except once a year on her birthday. She was not sure what the purpose of a hug was.

"Let me give you a hug. Sit there, Sarah. I've already made some eggs and toast, and here is your tea. Just relax. Don't worry. You've worked so hard, you poor little thing."

Before she could say anything, Jane carried on.

"Yes, I put the shopping away. You must have been so tired last night. I keep telling you that you are working too much."

She brought me breakfast and treated me like a princess. Maybe that's what I really need, a babysitter! She started to smile. *I do love Jane!*

What would she have done without her? When she had been on the point of crashing into depression, out of the blue, she had started visiting and bringing cookies and chatting and chatting. *I guess over the years she's learned to put up with me. It seemed not to bother her that I was not speaking too much and I was... just Sarah.*

Without replying, Sarah sat down and started eating, even though she was not hungry. You could not joke with Jane about food.

"Breakfast is important – you need to look after yourself."

"How are you today, Jane?"

Sarah actually enjoyed talking to her, even though it sometimes took her time to warm up in a conversation and she often managed only a few words.

Jane took a chair and brought her tea to the table. Looking at Sarah, she sat down and took her hand in hers.

"My dear, we need to talk."

Oh, no, that was the last thing she needed – another preaching about God and how much God loved her.

Where was God when my parents died? Where was God when I struggled with loneliness? Where was God when my heart was broken?

"Yes, yes," Jane had told her, "God is near to the broken-hearted," but she did not feel anyone with her in all her struggles.

Her thoughts were interrupted as Jane smiled and continued.

"I've spoken to Jim Carter. Our lovely preacher and his wife, Margaret. You met them before. I think it would be best for you to go and talk to them. They can help you. It has been so long now, Sarah. You need to do something about it... Girl, you are young and beautiful. It is time for you to move on with your life. Please, Sarah!"

"Jane, please don't start telling me again to go and see the preacher. How many times have we talked about this? It's Saturday and my house is a mess!"

She stood up from the chair. Was it really a mess? No. But she had to stop telling her to ask for help. For what?

"And I don't think I have time to go to church tomorrow. I have work to do. Look at all those papers over there!" She pointed to a tower of papers on the corner of a little coffee table.

Jane seemed not to be bothered by her attitude. It was not the first time she had spoken to Sarah, and she had learned how to deal with her over the years or put up with her wrestling and suffering in silence.

"Put God first and He will look after you. Submit your ways to the Lord and he will make straight your paths. My child, please go and see Jim and Margaret!"

As she leaned on the sink, Sarah felt tired of listening to the same old things. *If I go, she will leave me alone once and for all,* she thought. Suddenly, a warm feeling touched her heart. She felt a peace and a love that she'd never felt before. She was tired of fighting with the past and being angry with everything and everybody, even with God. Yes, with God.

For so long, nothing has happened. Maybe it happens for other people, but not for me, she argued.

But she turned to Jane and said with resignation, "Tomorrow, after church, I will speak to them both, OK?"

"That's my girl! You will see. Jim and Margaret are very kind, loving people and very wise. They will guide and help you, and you will find God's will for your life. All will be fine."

Sarah gave her a hug, which she didn't often do. She felt loved and cared for by this friend who had chosen to stand by her no matter what and not give up on her.

* * *

Work, work, work! And keep going without a purpose. That is how my life had ended up. Running away, wasn't it?

It was true, I was not fine, but each time I tried to move forward in life, it seemed I could not get anywhere and I was going backwards.

It was settled. But I did not want to go and get a lecture from Jim. But I had to do something. Maybe it would help. It was about God, and well, they were nice people.

Everyone around me treated me as though I was so naive and didn't know what was going on. They all had great ideas of what I should do and not do with my life. And yes, how to do it, as well.

But what about me, and what did I really want? What about me, about who I was? Tomorrow is tomorrow; it will be another day.

Chapter 2

First Step

Today was the day, Sunday! And Jane Marshall, with her beautiful simple dress and her purple coat, was waiting for me. It was raining and cold. It was the last Sunday in October and going to church was the last thing on my mind. If I had not promised, I might have tried to get out of it, but even excuses did not work with Jane these days.

"Why am I going with you today, Jane?"

"Because it's Sunday and we talked about it, Sarah. Come on, girl – get in the car. We don't want to be late. We'll take my car today. You look tired and need a break from driving." She kept pushing me, pushing me. She seldom gave up, but it seemed like I did. She had strength for me, sometimes.

I was dressed for going to the office; I did not even know what I should wear to church. How should I know? And I never was much into clothes or cared how I looked – what for? Did I really matter?

It was a quiet drive and in 20 minutes we were there. The church building was beautifully designed, and there were a lot of cars parked nicely. Many people said hello to me as if I was already their friend, which I did not understand. This was my fifth time or so, and it

---

Psalm 29:2
Ascribe to the Lord the glory due his name; worship the Lord in the splendor of holiness.

was hard for me to go. I preferred to be alone and I was not really interested in going to church or chatting, and definitely not making new friends. Too many people would make me anxious, and I did not like big gatherings. Jane knew that, for sure.

Grace Church was not a traditional Baptist Church or Anglican Church. It was the latest version of noise for me and it did not make sense to me. At least, not then. And there were so many people. Oh, my! I could not believe it... There must have been a few hundred. That was too much for me! Jane seemed popular as many people gave her hugs. She kept introducing me to people, and I kept smiling and saying hello.

"You remember my friend Sarah? She is my next-door neighbour and a lovely girl." I was not a girl, for sure. Did she know my age? I would be 35 the next year.

The main auditorium was huge, with lots of instruments at the front. I was hoping that Jane would not ask me to sit in the front row. I would have fainted. But Jane was very sensitive and guided me to the middle of the room where I felt I blended in with the huge crowd that invaded the room like ants.

The band was ready to make their "noise". There were lots of young people: Daniel, Mark, Thomas, Maria, Ruth and a few others. Jane had already told me all their names. They were the worship team, the Eagles, and they were all excellent musicians. Music, music and memories. I loved music. I loved singing. But that was long, long ago. I had not sung in years. But in my heart, there was still music. I always felt it could express your emotions, especially sadness, which was my best friend in that season of my life, but also joy, depending on how your emotions were playing you.

As worship started, I kept looking around, not sure what the procedure was and what I was supposed to do. Although I had been there before, change and new things always made me anxious. Some people were just standing quietly. For some reason, others were even sitting.

Are you serious, sitting? It seemed a bit rude to me, when more than half the building was up, worshipping and dancing. Not sure of what I wanted to do, I just sat quietly and tried to sing, but it was so embarrassing. I had only recently started singing in church.

Then I felt like closing my eyes and listening to the words: Jesus loves me, Jesus loves me, Jesus loves me.

Maybe that's why I came today, to hear those words that I am loved. Amazing! Then something else happened. My sad heart opened up a bit and was invaded by feelings of love and peace. It was good. Oh, my! It was like heaven!

I started smiling and feeling a bit joyful. I even danced a little. If my friends from work had seen me, they would have laughed. I did not dance. Period. I never knew how to dance. My parents always told me I was clumsy. Was I? Or afraid? Yet I loved music.

The more I sang, the more I connected with another world. I felt loved! All my worries were gone, and I felt, for the first time in my life, I could be *me*! Something was re-birthed in my heart, and maybe there was hope for me; maybe today would be a better day. And it *was* a better day. My heart was connecting with the Lord and the people around me.

Jane looked at me and out of the blue gave me a big hug. She whispered in my ear, "You've brought joy into my life. I love you, Sarah!"

After so many years of searching, I felt I'd found my place. Where was that? In a church! My heart had been searching for something unknown. For something more in this life than what I'd had to endure the past years. It must get better, mustn't it? Maybe for some, not for others. Going through a breakup and also the death of my parents, one after the other, kept hitting me, and I felt defeated by life and its circumstances. But that day, for the first time, I felt maybe there was a chance for me, maybe there was hope for something better in my life. What that would be I did not know.

* * *

The service was over. "What lovely preaching!" said a lady.

The Way, the Truth and the Life!

As in a dream, I left the building; guided by Jane, I sat in the car and became very quiet. I often used to do that. Jane drove me to the Carters' residence where they were expecting me.

How in the world they could drive there so quickly from church I never could figure out; maybe it was because I was too lost in my thoughts and lost track of time.

The main door opened.

"Hello, Sarah! How lovely to meet you again. Welcome to our home!" said the preacher.

"Yes, thank you for inviting me."

"Margaret and I are happy that you are joining us for lunch."

Margaret was a lovely lady in her mid-60s, like her husband. She was not very tall, had chestnut hair and was very quiet. She was simply and tastefully dressed.

Jim, on the other hand, was tall and very chatty. He was still dressed in the same shirt he had worn during the service.

For a moment, I felt embarrassed and did not know what to do. Going to new places always made me anxious. And yet I was working as a manager in a big company! I had started in advertising a few years previously and kept climbing, step by step, until I was offered the position of manager.

I loved my work and found it exciting to work with so many companies and people. I was competitive and driven and would work long hours. My job was my life. Or I did not have a life… Some people suspected I was running away from the past, hiding away or isolating myself. All of that was true, and deep down in my heart, I knew it. When pain and hurt and disappointment are too much to handle, some people try to find security in something that can never offer them the peace, love and fulfilment they are looking for. Although my job was good, my heart was burdened, and that imposed a lot of boundaries.

Jane started talking to Margaret, and they went into the kitchen to prepare some sandwiches for lunch. I was feeling really hungry when suddenly a voice behind me said politely, "Do go into the lounge."

The room was small and very comfortable. They were two couches facing each other, a long, narrow coffee table and a few armchairs arranged attractively.

A big glass window gave a beautiful view of a small conservatory full of beautiful, colourful flowering plants. I could not keep mine alive for even a week. Either I would not water them, or I would give them too much water. Plants were not my thing.

Around the room hung large, colourful paintings that took you back in time. I felt as though I was travelling through history.

Suddenly I saw a big mirror on the wall, and I noticed someone in it.

Yes, it was me. It was Sarah Grant.

You could tell I did not look in a mirror. Maybe I was afraid of what I might see. It was such a long time since I'd looked in a mirror. Where was it in my home? Oh, yes, now I remember. I had one in the hall behind the front door. Who was Sarah Grant? That was a very good question.

I saw shoulder-length chestnut hair, a round face, big, sparkling green eyes, a very fine chin and a lovely smile. Yes, I had a lovely smile; I was always told that. I was not very tall and I was not much in fashion, but I wasn't ugly. Actually, I was beautiful. To think I was beautiful – that was quite something. I'd been told that before but never believed it. I'd always believed that everyone was beautiful in their own way, but I'd never thought about myself.

Who am I? That was a very good question, and I could not answer it.

My thoughts were interrupted by Jim, who entered the lounge and start a conversation.

"Sarah, first, I thank you that you came. We have been praying for you."

"Thank you," I whispered.

"Jane talks a lot about you. She is very fond of you and always tells us what a good girl you are. I understand that you must have passed through some very difficult moments, losing your parents in such tragic circumstances. I am so sorry. I just want you to know that Jesus loves you and He is here with you. And we are here, too, and if you want to talk to me or Margaret, please do not hesitate to call us and come by for a cup of tea. It would be a pleasure to have you here. Our house is an open house, and we love having friends over. Jane will tell you that too."

He smiled and the conversation continued. It was not the hour's preaching I'd expected or a questionnaire about my life. We talked about all kinds of things, from church worship to Margaret's garden, the weather and my work. I started to relax and gradually joined in.

Jim gave me a Bible that he had brought into the room earlier.

"Read it when you have time and meditate. It will help you more than I will ever do." He smiled.

I was totally confused. I'd expected to be treated like a psychologist's patient, as if I was the problem and needed to be fixed. Wasn't it like that? Everyone wanted to change everything and everybody. How can you be yourself in a world that changes all the time and wants to change you? *Now, what next?* I thought.

Jane and Margaret brought in the food and we all enjoyed the sandwiches. I had to admit that I was glad that I'd come.

Margaret told a story about the cat which stole a piece of fish from the kitchen and how she'd accused Jim of eating it. They all laughed.

Soon it was 4 pm, and before leaving, Jane asked Jim to pray for us.

Finally, the moment of truth for me, and I could see how people prayed.

"Dear Father, thank you for a lovely time and for being with us and always providing for us. We thank you for our new friend Sarah, and we ask you to be with us and bless us throughout the coming week."

This was a very simple prayer. I had thought they would do something more complicated. But it was from the heart. There was no ritual, no rules; it was simple and sincere.

* * *

Home, sweet home. Finally, we were home, and I told Jane I was tired and had to catch up with some work as the following day there was a big presentation for one of the projects. I had to re-evaluate the work that had been done so it could be launched.

My house was quiet and it seemed lonely. It was dark outside and I could hear the wind. I noticed the Bible that Jim had given me, and I took it upstairs with all the paperwork from the office.

I was not in the mood to work at my desk, and I just threw everything in the middle of my big bed. The colours of my room were so dark and it was such a dark room that I had to turn on the lights all the time. The only light was from a large window which I loved. That was where I put my little desk and where I usually worked.

But now I felt tired, and I was thinking about everything that had happened. I felt it had been a good day after all. I felt accepted and nobody had asked me questions or made me do anything... I could just be me. And I had not asked anything, either. I was just happy to be at Jim's house with some friends.

As scenes came into my mind, I got caught up again in the past…

The school had organized a singing contest, which gave everybody an opportunity to sing. My best friend, Maria, and I were very excited, and we managed to convince our parents to let us participate. It took us a few weeks to prepare, and I had to do some extra chores as if I was being punished by my parents. That is how it felt, just to be allowed to sing in a school contest.

The contest was a fundraising event for the school. Throughout the summer, the school organized art competitions, athletic events, and all sorts of things to raise funds. Sadly, my parents did not care much for sport or the arts, so for me to convince them to let me participate in the Musical Event was quite a big thing.

They kept telling me over and over that I would fail, that I should not go, that it was not for me. I usually listened to them, but for some reason this time, I did not. I really loved singing, and I worked hard practising a song I loved. I had to hide when I did this as my parents thought it distracted me from studying or my chores. I can still remember my little pink dress. It was the first big thing in my life.

The competition was held on a lovely morning in July, but like everything in my life, nothing came easy. It started good but ended up bad.

All the children and their parents were asked to be at the school by 2 pm. We were there at 1.30 pm. Till the last minute, my parents were fearful and worried. They kept telling me I would make myself a fool and I should not be there. I loved my parents, but for some reason, they worried about everything. Sometimes I was overwhelmed by criticism. I could not do anything right, and they were never pleased with anything I did. But I was determined to sing.

All the parents found seats in a large auditorium and waited for the event to start. There was a big stage with curtains and a large poster saying Musical Event.

There were 10 children competing, and we were each given a number. One by one, we took our turn. Five teachers were the judges, and they were going to choose the best five singers. It took longer than two hours as we had breaks and the music had to be set up for each child.

Marie was number four, and she sang pretty well. I was so pleased for her. She was my best friend and the only friend my parents let me have. I was number seven, and I had to wait. I could see my parents were not relaxed; they were not good at handling big gatherings like this. I was hoping they would settle down by the time I finally sang.

They never shared much with me about their lives, but they were always fearful: afraid of people, afraid of gatherings and afraid that something bad would happen to them and me and everyone. I never understood them, but their behaviour and lifestyle impacted my childhood and still impacts my life to this day.

When my turn came, I went onto the stage and started to sing. I wanted my parents to be pleased, but they looked more and more worried. Was I singing badly, or was something wrong with my pink dress? What was the problem now?

When I finished singing, the people applauded and I felt excited and appreciated. As I was enjoying the moment, my parents suddenly stood up, and as soon as I'd left the stage, they took me by the hand and took me home. It was so embarrassing in front of my entire school and all my friends. At home, I hid and cried for days.

Later I found out that I had been awarded third place and won a prize, which was amazing. My classmates and the teachers told me, but because of my parents rushing off, I could never enjoy my little victory.

* * *

I blinked a few times, and I was back in my room facing a pile of papers. I sat on the bed and took one of the files. I was not in the mood for reading through the whole project. The next morning Richard would say, "Did you read it? I need to present it," and on and on. Richard was my right-hand man, my second in command. We had worked together for the past five years. I had a good team and was responsible for around 100 people, which was quite challenging at times, but I liked my job.

As I took another file, I saw the Bible that Jim had given to me and I opened it. You would think I would start at the beginning, but I opened it at John chapter 3. I read it once and then again and again. There was something about this Bible. I could not understand what I was reading, but I felt that it was answering some of my questions.

I eventually fell asleep with the Bible in the middle of all my files. I woke up during the night, only to put all the files on the floor and go back to sleep. Tomorrow would be a busy day.

Chapter 3

Moving on

It was Monday morning and she did not even need an alarm, though she had two set in the house to make sure she was not late for work. She had noisy, old-fashioned clocks which had belonged to her parents.

Sarah was always at work by 8.30, sometimes even at 8.00, and was there before anyone else. Richard often said that she was checking up on them, but that was not true. She liked to set an example, and she also had a tremendous amount of work to do. And for her, being at work was better than being at home.

One by one, the staff came in. The office was a big room divided into little "cells", and the people were all chatting like busy bees. Sarah's office was separate, and she was already there, working and looking at her agenda.

"Morning, Sarah. I told you not to come so early!" Richard showed up as usual. He was a tall, handsome man with dark hair and dark eyes and was very chatty.

"Good morning, Richard. Did you have a good weekend?"

---

1 John 4:6
We are from God. Whoever knows God listens to us; whoever is not from God does not listen to us. By this we know the Spirit of truth and the spirit of error.

He sat on the chair in front of Sarah and started talking. Even if Sarah had her nose in her files or was looking at her laptop, she listened to Richard. It had become a habit for him to confess his weekend sins and share his adventures and failures.

"You know, Sarah, I went to Tina's house over the weekend. You would not believe it. We had a party and invited like half of the office... "

"Yes, Richard, and how is Tina?"

"Tina's fine. I think she is eating too much and for sure drinking too much. We talked about splitting up."

" Again?" Sarah asked and she lifted her eyes from the files.

Richard stood up and started pacing from one corner of the room to another. "We have been together for two years now, but I am kind of getting bored with her, and she is drinking too much. Maybe I should have dated someone like you."

Sarah was not surprised by his comments. She was not the type of girl to be impressed by that type of talk. It was the same conversation every Monday morning. The man had to talk to somebody and tell someone his problems regarding Tina, and there you go, Sarah was nice enough to listen. Sarah was so good at listening to many of her colleagues that some said she was in the wrong job. She was a good listener, it's true, but sorting out people's problems was not her job, and she had quite enough on her heart and mind. In a kind but authoritative voice, Sarah said, "Richard, let's get back to work, and we can talk about Tina later!"

Sarah was a very gentle manager at Creative Ideas and had coordinated this team for more than two years. Some time ago, she had been offered a higher position and would have had to move to London, but she refused it. She liked what she was doing. The salary was pretty good and she could afford more things in her life, but for the past few years, she'd kept saving and saving, doing nothing much, just burying herself in her work. It kept her going, and she started erecting barriers around herself, putting boundaries around her heart to guard herself as she was afraid to get out.

Richard changed his posture, straightened his blue suit, smiled and said, "Yes, Boss."

Sarah handed him a list of the main things that needed looking after that day. "I have five meetings, and I need all the projects to be ready. I will start with the Aurora project, and we need to launch it." She went on to the Kids Campaign, then Helping Cats, then Saving Lives.

The phone rang and Richard knew that was time to start moving. He left the office.

"Yes, Sarah Grant speaking. Yes, yes, I will try to organize it for tomorrow. Please talk to my secretary and she will sort it out. Yes... thank you."

A few minutes later, she walked out of her office. She was a different kind of manager from all the others. She liked to spend the time from 10 am till 12 noon supporting all the other employees who were working on various projects and advising them. She believed in teamwork and encouraging the staff to achieve their best.

She walked passed Sonia, who had worked for the company for many years and was very good at her job. Creative Ideas had started with a small office, and now the big bosses in London wanted to extend it. Since they could not move Sarah out of Abilene, they decided to build a big building and move everyone from the current little building into the new one when it was ready. The project was still in construction, and the plans were that the following year they would move into the big fancy building. It was only 10 minutes away from this one.

"Sarah, I've heard from Kids Campaign. They want us to organize two platforms of fundraising and also to advertise on three levels. Shall I organize my team of 10 and look into it? What do you have in mind?"

"Let me see," said Sarah. She took a chair and looked at the main ideas and presentations. "Yes, that would be fine. Make sure you take the new girl with you. I do not want her to feel lost in any way and she needs to learn. Take her under your wing and teach her. Make sure she is not alone at lunch. She just started last week."

"Yes, Sarah!"

Suddenly Richard appeared from nowhere.

"Are you coming to the meeting for the Aurora project? It is a very good virtual presentation, but Mike's team is struggling with the figures... It seems the cost is too high and they need it cut by 20%. Shall I do another cost spreadsheet?"

Sarah took the files from Richard and walked to one of the three main meetings rooms where the project was being presented.

"Hello everyone. I am Sarah Grant."

"The manager!" whispered Richard.

She never liked to present herself as a manager. She wanted to be able to interact with people according to their needs and how the company could help them. Pleasant negotiation and a good contract for both sides would make everyone happy.

"I understand that the cost is too high. Let's see what we can do for you!"   She looked at the cost spreadsheet and asked Mike to spread it over six months. "We could offer you 20% off the actual price and spread it over six months instead of three. Would that make things easier?"

Everyone seemed happy and the contract was signed.

During her break, Sarah went outside for a minute. While sitting in the park, she looked at the sky. *Where are you, God? I would like to talk to you*, she thought. Spending time thinking of heaven and God was quite unusual for her as she had all kinds of projects going on in her mind.

Usually, she would go out with a colleague for lunch, but today she wanted to be alone and appreciate nature around her. This was also quite unusual, as she loved keeping things the same and having a schedule and some stability.

The rest of the day passed with phone calls and more projects to be verified and organized, and by the time she'd finished, it was 5 pm.

Jane, as usual, was at the door, and she kept talking.

Sometimes it was tiring listening to her. Did she ever get tired of talking? She would never be able to talk so much. But she could not imagine Jane otherwise.

"How are you, Sarah? You look tired. Shall I order Chinese?"

"Yes, please. I am definitely not cooking tonight."

Jane immediately ordered some food, and in less than 30 minutes it was delivered.

"Let me tell you my news, Sarah, and how busy I was today. I met Margaret again as we went and helped an elderly lady. She is so sweet, but sadly she cannot come to church, so we try to help and visit as often as we can. I also went and met Miriam, my friend, for a cup of tea. She told me that her children are moving away and she was sad. And yes... my neighbour asked me if she could come to church with me. Is that not wonderful?!"

"Yes, it is. You have been quite busy."

Sarah looked around and felt the need to talk.

"You know, Jane, for so many years now you have looked after me and kept me company. You cook for me, and you help me tidy up my house. You even take me to church now. You are so good to me. I'm really grateful, and I am so glad you are here. My life without you would have been quite lonely. And it has started to make a bit more sense since I met you."

Jane had tears in her eyes and gave her a big hug, which made Sarah feel good. Don't tell me that she'd started to enjoy hugs! Well, that was something new, but Grace Church was a bunch of people that loved hugs.

"You are my family, Jane!"

Looking in her eyes, she carried on.

"I have been thinking about going and talking with Jim and Margaret again and seeing whether I can somehow move on with my life as I feel I have been stuck in time since my parents died. What do you think?"

She was not sure when she'd made that decision, but she had to do something and felt that both Jim and Margaret would be able to help her and guide her step by step. They would stand by her and she would not feel pushed or forced into doing anything but walk the walk of her new life.

Jane was so surprised she did not know what to say.

"Yes, of course. It would be a very good idea. You are young, beautiful and intelligent and you have a good heart. I think it is time for you to move on, and they will help you. Jim is a godly man, and when I lost my husband, he and his wife helped me to move on with my life. Let's take it a step at a time and see."

"I might give them a call tomorrow."

"Let me know if I can help with anything, my child!"

They finished their dinner in silence, and Sarah felt she was finally moving in the right direction. Things were moving slowly, and she felt the Lord was shining a light in her life and the sun was rising for her too. For the first time in a long time, there was hope in her heart of a better life. It was not that she was starving, but the new beginning, the new door opened, would bring new friends, new desires, new dreams.

Chapter 4

Help me, please!

A few weeks had passed since I'd met Jim and Margaret Carter, and I was invited to meet them on a rainy Saturday in November.

Jane was making sure I went to church with her and did not work so much. Honestly, I started to enjoy my Sundays, and they became my favourite day of the week. It was something I could not explain, but being in the house of the Lord made me feel loved. That love would carry me through the week, and then I'd go back for more.

This time, I was not invited to their home but invited to meet them at the church. It was a beautiful modern building, and in the parking area were a few cars of volunteers helping in the church. They were always doing something, and it amazed me how they had time to work a full-time job, raise kids, look after their house and help at the church.

The building had a big lobby with a large room for coffee and cake and then entrances to various rooms for kids' activities, bible study groups and other ministries. It was strange to see the chairs and the stage empty.

Jim came out from a small office on the right side of the building and apologized.

Psalm 54:4
Behold, God is my helper; the Lord is the upholder of my life.

"Hello, Sarah. So sorry that you have to wait. I am afraid Margaret had to leave due to an emergency phone call. One of the ladies from the church was taken to hospital."

"No problem. Today I am free, so I can wait."

Jim apologised again and continued.

"I am sorry I am also a bit caught up for 15 more minutes, so would you mind waiting a bit longer?"

"No problem. It's OK, please do not worry. I will be here when you are finished."

"That's good... that's good. Thank you."

Jim left and I found myself in the middle of the large room. As I walked closer to the front, I noticed that the instruments were on the stage but nobody was there. How exciting to be on the stage! I walked slowly up the steps and looked at all the beautiful instruments and the microphone. They must have just finished their practice.

I looked all around the auditorium and there was only me. As I approached the microphone, I remembered when I was young, singing!

Me, singing. Yes, I loved to sing but never sang as lead singer; I was a kind of background singer. And I loved singing when I was at university, with a small group of friends. It was too much for me to be up on a stage, even if my friends insisted I try. I could perform in front of them but not in a room full of hundreds of people.

My parents were never up for the dream of music, which I had considered for a while. They were not the best at encouraging me. Yes, that was a long-ago dream of mine, to sing in a band, and now I was on a stage with a microphone and could sing without anyone seeing me. Why not?

Without hesitation, I picked up the microphone and felt a boldness and a courage that I'd never felt before. I'd forgotten how much I loved music and singing. Me, the boss, the manager, Jane's next-door neighbour – on a stage.

A few people entered the room but I did not notice. They were the main Eagles worship band: Daniel, the lead singer, and Mark, Thomas, Maria and Ruth, who were vocals and instruments.

I took the microphone and held it tight. Then I closed my eyes, let myself get carried away and started singing.

What was I singing – a Christian song?

Yes, and I did not even realise it. I'd obviously learnt the first few verses over the past few weeks. I kept singing them over and over again, more and more confidently, with my eyes closed. It was like being carried away by the Spirit and led into something new, like a dream re-birthing in a different way.

Then I heard the instruments and realised the others were there. I got scared and stopped. I turned around and saw all of them waving at me and telling me to keep going.

Then I heard somebody else singing with me. About 2 meters from me was Daniel. I started panicking and did not know what to do. Embarrassed, I put my head down and turned to leave.

"So sorry, I should not have done that!" I managed to say.

"Please stay! You have a beautiful voice," said a kind voice behind me. Daniel was waiting to see my reaction, and everyone was looking at me.

Should I go or should I stay?

Then I did something totally out of character. I turned around and walked back toward the microphone. Daniel handed me the microphone and with a nod and a smile encouraged me to sing. He showed me where the words and music were.

I was not sure whether I would remember how to sing, but there were only a few of them and no people in the room to make me feel embarrassed.

The drums started and then the guitar came in, and Daniel started to sing. I was not sure how to do it... but after a few minutes, as he was prompting me, I got the idea of how to follow the song and managed to sing.

Can you imagine, me singing? After so many years! What would my parents say if they saw me here? What would my colleagues say if they saw me singing in a church?

Unaware of the time, I sang for more than 20 minutes.

A few chairs in the main auditorium were taken, and I noticed that even Jim was there. For the first time, I was not totally embarrassed, and I actually enjoyed myself. After an hour, the practice came to an end.

"I did not know you could sing, Sarah?" Mark said.

"You must be Jane Marshall's neighbour. She talks about you with everyone!"

"Yes, that's me! I am so sorry, I should not have taken over the stage like this."

Daniel apologised as he was in a rush. He received a phone call and he left in a hurry, saying goodbye to all of us.

"Don't mind him," said Maria. "He is always running! He runs a construction company and he is all over the place. I am surprised he still has time to sing and serve in the worship team."

Thomas joined them as well.

"He loves music and is quite passionate about worship. He is the heart of our team. He is quite something! Without him, we would be nothing, in a way."

I did not know what to say, so I smile and apologised again for jumping on the stage.

"Hey, Sarah, you are full of surprises," said Jim. "You have a beautiful voice and other wonderful gifts that you could use in the church as well."

He invited me to go into another room where there were two armchairs and a little table, and we had a cup of tea and started talking.

"So, how can I help you today, Sarah?"

I looked down at my shoes. I was not sure how to start and I fidgeted with my hands. Jim noticed I was very anxious and carried on.

"You do not need to worry, Sarah. You are in a safe place. The Lord brought you here and the Lord will carry you and help you. I am here just to guide you. This is a private conversation."

"Actually, I had been thinking the past few weeks about giving my life to the Lord!"

Jim was totally surprised as he listened to my words.

"I am not the best with big gatherings of people, but I would love to get baptised in church and have a small group of friends."

Jim's eyes were sparkling.

"Sarah, this is the best decision you could ever take! Starting the journey with the Lord will be very rewarding. I am not saying it will be easy, but it will be a journey where you will have the Lord with you. Your life will be on a new road, and the Lord will transform and change you. And yes, the beautiful helper, the Holy Spirit!"

We went into the details of when to be baptised and decided on the following Saturday, with just a few people from church. However, it would be announced in the church as I would be a new member of Christ's family.

"Thank you, Pastor Jim, for all your help. Let me take it slowly and see what the next step for me is. I do want to move on with my life, and I need help."

"OK, Sarah, you tell me when are ready to move on, and we'll take it slowly. I will pray about it and see how we can help you as a church."

On the way home in the car, I thought about my little music adventure. It had been really good and I felt so blessed. All kinds of unexpected things had happened lately, and it felt as though the Lord was calling me and challenging me to try old and new things.

Jane was waiting for me as usual. She was actually in my house, and as soon as she heard the car parked, she opened the front door.

"Come child, come, you must be hungry. I organized a late lunch for us and was thinking we could watch a film."

Always the good Jane being there for me and pushing me more and more, even when I wanted to do nothing. That lovely old lady, she kept going as if she was never tired.

"Yes, Jane, I am coming."

Inside, we made ourselves comfortable on the couch and the film started on the TV. Out of the blue, I said, "Jane, I am getting baptised next Saturday!"

Jane looked at me.

"Really, Sarah, I can't believe it! What made you decide to do this?"

"I want to be part of God's big, lovely family, like this, where I feel loved."

I was looking forward to starting my new journey with the Lord. I felt I was at the beginning of something beautiful, hard and challenging, but I was willing to try.

Chapter 5

My home?

It was already December and a few weeks had passed since Sarah had been baptised. Her week was busy with her advertising and fundraising projects and weekends were spent with Jane and the church.

She had joined the Eagles, only for practice, even if the team kept asking her to sing during Sunday service.

That was too much for her, so she just enjoyed singing with them and making new friends. Jane was as busy as ever, took Sarah on her visits to older ladies who could not come to church, and started teaching her all kinds of things.

Oh, yes. Sarah joined a little home group on Wednesdays and she loved it. The first time she went, she was a bit nervous and did not even know what she was doing there. She thought that she would get a Bible teaching and a lecture. However, Wendy and Peter Duncan were a very nice couple in their late 50s. They introduced Sarah to the small group of seven people, some of whom she remembered from church.

Philippians 1:6
And I am sure of this, that he who began a good work in you will bring it to completion at the day of Jesus Christ.

Her first home group meeting turned out to be very good. They had sandwiches and tea and a lovely chat. Then they had prayers and a short Bible verse. That was how the Duncans did it. Other groups might have been a bit different. However, that was all Sarah needed to be able to keep going and start on her journey with the Lord.

Her focus gradually changed. She managed to dress a bit better than just wearing her office clothes, and she was able to relax, not bringing any more work home. Her weekend was treasured, and she started to enjoy herself. She also developed a good daily routine of spending time with the Lord.

If you had known Sarah, you would know that she was not very talkative and did not share her emotions, but slowly she was learning to open up. She started to not only praise the Lord and be thankful but draw near Him and discover how much she was loved by the Lord. She loved reading her Bible, and even her colleagues at work told her she'd changed and looked happier and more relaxed.

Although she was more settled, she was still living in that old house full of memories, and in a way, she wanted to move now more than ever.

She started to pray and ask the Lord about many things, and one of them was her parents' house, her home.

What shall I do my Lord? Shall I sell the house?

Jim invited her for tea at their house, and she was eager to visit them again. They helped her so much. She felt at home there, and they were always kind and welcoming.

"Hey, Sarah, you are here... good. You know your way and Margaret will bring the tea. We'll have a lovely chat, shall we?"

Margaret was a very patient lady who always listened to her and had a lovely smile on her face.

"How are you, Sarah?"

"Thank you, Margaret, I am very well! I wanted to come and talk to you as there is something on my heart."

"Of course, of course."

Jim came into the lounge as well, and both were excited to hear what Sarah had to say.

"As you know, the Lord had been so good to me and brought me from far away home. However, I feel that the Lord wants me to start afresh."

Margaret looked at Jim and interrupted.

"Of course you came from far away. Look at you singing on Saturdays, Sarah, and you have such a lovely voice. It would be great if you could find the courage to start singing on a Sunday."

Sarah smiled.

"You need to ask the Lord as I get extremely anxious, and doing that would be a big thing for me. However, I love the home group, and Peter and Wendy have been very kind and patient with me. Thank you for encouraging me to join a house group. Now, why I came today is because it has been on my heart to sell the house and move into a new house."

"Really, Sarah? What made you think of it?"

Margaret poured some tea into pretty, decorative cups.

"I want a fresh start in every area in my life. A few years ago, I lost my parents in a car crash, but that is not all. My parents were lovely people and very kind, but they never encouraged me in singing or anything I wanted to do. They had a different approach to life and they seemed afraid of people and challenges. As a child, I was limited to one best friend. No birthday parties, not even activities. I was always at home, as if I was hidden away. I never knew why or what had happened in their lives, but I felt like a girl in a cage. One day I realized I was living my life to please them and not doing anything I wanted to do. I loved my parents, but I'd never been able to please them. After I lost them in the accident, I realized I was trapped in the past, in a house full of memories, and could not go on. I want to go on. I want a fresh start. I want to do the things I want to do, go where I want to go. Dress how I want, eat how I want... find out who I am! I am 35 years old and I do not know myself."

Jim and Margaret were pleased with her approach and they prayed with her.

"Now, Sarah, let's see what the Lord wants to do. But first, you will need to forgive and let go of the past."

"OK, this is new for me. Lots of memories of all kinds come and go. What shall I do with them?"

"You need to give it all to the Lord. Give it to Jesus and He will heal you."

"OK, I am listening, Jim."

"You need to forgive your parents and people that hurt you. You need to let go of them and give them to Jesus. This is a process, and it might take some time. For some people, it takes months, for others a bit longer. Only the Lord knows each one's heart. Ask the Lord to help you, and each time hurtful memories come into your mind, just speak out loud and say, 'I surrender. I forgive them,' and let go. Talk to the Lord, and the Holy Spirit will teach you and guide you."

"Why would I need to do that repeatedly? Is once not enough?

"The Lord is taking on your past, Sarah, and is very patient with you! From what you shared today, I believe that your parents were too protective and controlling. You need to let the Lord guide you and carry you through the entire healing process."

Sarah thought for a minute and tears ran down her cheeks.

Margaret came and gave her a big hug.

"You are not responsible for your parents and the way they treated you. You are not responsible for anyone. You are responsible for yourself."

Jim paused and smiled at Sarah.

"I know it is not easy, but when you go home, think and pray about it and the Lord will give you His wisdom grace and reveal His will. As I said, He will carry you through."

"So, you're telling me that I have to keep surrendering my parents and other people that hurt me to the Lord, as many times as needed? And one day it won't hurt anymore. There will just be some memories and scars."

"Yes, Sarah, and the Lord will heal you. The scars will still be there, but you will get beauty for ashes."

"This is quite a lot to take in and I will need time to meditate on it. But may I ask one more question?"

Jim smiled as she always had lots of questions, and sometimes it took them three or four hours to talk to her. They were dedicated to helping her and anyone else who was bold enough to ask for help.

"Yes, Sarah?"

"What do I need to forgive them for?"

"For the way they treated you and the hurt they caused you, knowingly or unknowing. It is the only way, to go to the cross and let God work in your life. Your heart and your mind will be relieved. It's not because they deserve it; none of us does. But the Lord, in His infinite mercy, gave his Son for us. He died for all of us. We are all sinners. Who forgives much will love much, Sarah. The Lord is gracious to all of us, and how much more should we, his beloved children, learn to follow in his footsteps. The Lord knows what you went through, everything in your life, unfair or hurtful, and He calls you at the cross and says, 'Give it to me, as I died on the cross for you, so you can have life and have it abundantly.' His Spirit will guide you and His love embraces you. You are not alone. The Lord will carry you through, and we are here with you too."

Sarah's large tears were trickling down her cheeks, but in the middle of this beautiful conversation, her phone rang. She did not want to take the call but then apologised and answered. "Yes, Sarah speaking."

She stood up with a horrified expression and a few seconds later hung up the phone. "My house has been robbed!"

Jim and Margaret tried to calm her down, but she was scared and she whooshed out the door, apologising and promising she would meditate on the conversation.

When she parked on the driveway, there were a couple of police cars and Jane. She found out that everything had been smashed as the thieves searched for jewellery and cash.

"I had 100 pounds in cash and I do not have jewellery, except two old rings from my parents."

That was the truth. She'd never had any jewellery or anything like that as her parents were against it, and she did not have anything valuable in the house, except her heart. Her heart and memories were in the house.

The policemen took another statement and after 15 minutes they left.

It was dark and cold. She went inside and looked around. It started to rain and she felt so lonely. She was scared and in shock. She could not say one word.

Everything was in pieces. Dishes and other items had been thrown on the floor and broken; even in her bedroom, they'd made a mess. Who it was and why it had happened she did not understand, but she could not stay there. She shivered. She had to go and sleep somewhere else that night; then in the morning she would see what needed to be done.

Jane touched her gently on the shoulder.

"I have a spare room in my small bungalow. Would you like me to help you pack some clothes? Come over to my house. Let's lock the door, and we will see what needs to be done tomorrow."

As in a dream, Sarah packed a few things, prompted by Jane. She just wanted to leave as soon as possible, get out of the house, get out of her mind, get out of everything that was past.

Jane's house was lovely, full of colour and flowery curtains, flowery teacups, everything with flower patterns. A big orange cat welcomed her.

Sarah had often been to Jane's house, but this time she was more than grateful to be there. She did not know where she belonged and felt confused and tired.

She told Jane she wanted to sleep and went quietly to bed. Now was the time when she drew closer to the Lord, took her Bible and found peace and comfort in His Word. Her fear and worry slowly ebbed away, and she kept reading until she fell asleep.

She could hear Jane making phone calls and talking to Jim and a few others. Tomorrow was Sunday, after all, and what better place to be than at church?

Chapter 6

One more step

It was already morning, and I woke up feeling better. Sitting on the edge of the bed, I remembered my conversation with Jim and Margaret about letting go of the past and forgiving. I did not understand much, but I would have done anything to have some peace and get rid of the memories and nightmares that had haunted me for years.

Jane was already dressed for church, and she even cooked some breakfast. I told her I would have a shower and get ready.

As the water fell on my face in the shower, I looked down and remembered "He shed his blood." My lovely Saviour died for me so I would have a better life. Tears flowed down my face and in my heart was a deep pain that I could not get rid of. After some time, I heard Jane's voice telling me to hurry as we would be late for church. I managed to dress and move, but my thoughts were somewhere else.

"You are quiet today, Sarah. Don't worry, my girl, I spoke with Jim last night, and we are your family; we'll look after you."

I was feeling sad and I was not sure what to do about it.

---

1 John 1:9
If we confess our sins, he is faithful and just to forgive us our sins and to cleanse us from all unrighteousness.

There was too much coming and going in my life, and meeting people in circumstances like that was not always the best idea. At least not for me.

"Not sure I should go to church today with you, Jane. I feel down. And so many things are going on; it feels too much...."

Jane looked at me, worried.

"Child, we will go to church together. It will be all right!" and she gave me a big hug. Jane and her hugs always made me feel better. She treated me like her daughter. Or at least that was how I felt once I got to know her better.

Maybe it would be all right, but it was not easy. The Lord was doing some work in my heart, gently, and was kind of pushing me an extra step. It was hard to take the first step, but once outside the door, I felt I could breathe more easily.

It might have been the fresh air after the rain that we'd had during the night and the burdens being lifted from my shoulders by Jesus.

Pale rays of sunshine were struggling through the clouds, and a refreshing little breeze was blowing through my hair.

As I looked at the sky, I thought, *New beginning for me, new house!*

As we stepped into the building, Jim and Margaret were waiting for me to make sure I was all right after the break-in.

He was dressed in his best Sunday suit and had his big Bible in his hand. He had lots of written papers and he seemed to be in a hurry.

"Hello Sarah, how are you? Jane spoke to us last night."

Trying to smile, I answered in a very calm voice that surprised even me. "I am fine thank you, Jim. I guess now I do have to move!"

He glanced at his watch and touched my shoulder:

"Listen, girl, I'll leave you with Margaret, as I have to get ready. I am preaching today. We'll talk more after service, shall we?"

As he left, Margaret took over and was kind, as always.

"Sarah, would you like to come over to our house after the church service? We can talk and see how we can help you. We've invited some friends from church – hope that is OK with you. What do you say?"

For sure, I did not want to go home, so I accepted the invitation gratefully. Usually, in circumstances like that, I would prefer to be alone, but this time, I did not. I wanted to be among friends.

The music started and it was loud. My heart started to beat so strongly that I was afraid someone would hear it. As I sat down, my eyes went straight to the worship group.

Something arose in my heart: joy. The joy of the Lord was my strength. It grew and grew as I listened to the music. Amazing grace flowing through the room and into people's hearts.

It was the same Eagles band that I spent so many Saturdays with. Mark lead the first two songs. It was an amazing team. Even though Daniel was the main singer, there were lots of people involved. It was not focused on one person. It was Christ-focused and beautiful worship, all for God's glory.

As I was standing and singing, some people were happy and bouncy, but I felt more humbled and quiet in my heart. I would not jump and bounce anyway; that was definitely not me.

The worship was usually for 30-40 minutes and was good and uplifting. I'd also heard from Jane that there were lots of prayer and intercessors' groups in the morning at 9:30, but I'd never participated in one. Not yet.

For the third song, Daniel stepped in front, and for the first time, I noticed him. He was tall and had dark blonde hair. His eyes were of a deep ocean blue. He was wearing a dark blue T-shirt and jeans. That was more his style, I would say.   He always surprised me with his free style of dressing.

As the song started, I remembered the previous Saturday morning and their singing practice. I had started looking forward to singing and having fun. Ruth was always chatty, and Thomas always had new ideas and loved playing with notes. My mind raced back.

"Hey Sarah, what do you think about this song?" Daniel walked onto the stage and handed me a few pages with the words and music.

"Yes, it is good..." I replied.

Daniel turned toward Thomas and said, "Let's move it up, Thomas; otherwise it will be too slow. You know me by now."

"What do you say, Sarah, shall we sing together?" He smiled at me and brought his microphone closer. "I did not print enough copies, so we can share."

I looked at him, not sure what to do. I was getting used to his very direct manner. It was a bit much at the beginning, but I'd learned that Daniel was a very bold, confident and fun person. Much like the name of the band, he was an eagle – he was always filled with joy and always persevered. He kept me on my toes with new ideas and songs.

"I'll be your echo!" I offered.

"No, sing with me, please." He looked straight into my eyes and did not move.

Ruth was laughing and told me, "When Daniel says something, you better listen, girl! He does not understand NO very well!"

But even when the instruments played and Daniel started singing, I just could not sing. He had a beautiful, powerful voice. He had a confidence and a passion for singing, and that was worship, when you put your heart into it. For a moment, I just admired him, then felt shy.

He raised his hand and the music stopped.

"Why are you not singing? What's wrong with the song? Don't you like it?"

I looked down, confused.

Then he said in a very soft voice, "Please sing with me. It took me three hours last night to choose this song. Just for you to sing with me." It sounded like begging, but in a bold voice.

He raised his hand, and the band started again. I looked at him in surprise and joined him singing. What a beautiful song.

However, right now, he was singing the song alone on the stage. It was so beautiful, and I wished I was up there, singing with him.

Not everyone could sing, and not everyone sang with passion, but it was something that Daniel was pretty good at. I'd had a chance to join the band but had refused over and over to sing on Sundays, and now they might not even ask me anymore.

In the middle of the song, while I was dreaming away, I noticed Daniel was looking at me. I felt embarrassed, and the moment our eyes met, I looked down. But Daniel kept looking at me during the song. I wished I had not been so shy and had agreed to sing on Sundays. I went back to my thoughts about singing on stage or quitting.

Then I heard Jim begin his sermon, and it was about Martha and Mary – Luke 10:38-42.

"Now as they went on their way, Jesus entered a village. And a woman named Martha welcomed him into her house. And she had a sister called Mary, who sat at the Lord's feet and listened to his teaching. But Martha was distracted with much serving. And she went up to him and said, 'Lord, do you not care that my sister has left me to serve alone? Tell her then to help me.' But the Lord answered her, 'Martha, Martha, you are anxious and troubled about many things, but one thing is necessary. Mary has chosen the good portion, which will not be taken away from her.'"

It was exactly what I needed to hear: "Do not worry."

"The Lord is good. The Lord is kind. The Lord is merciful. The Lord knows your heart. You should not hide from the Lord, no matter in what situation you are or what you are going through because the Lord loves you.

"The Lord is your loving Father and he wants to hear your voice, to see your face and for you to invite Him into your problems, into your house, into your family. Let Him fully know your heart. The truth will set you free.

"The Lord is near the broken-hearted and hears their cry and heals them.

"The Lord is a good Father, and it might take time, but He will carry you through. He will deliver you and give you beauty for ashes. Mary, Martha and Lazarus were friends of Jesus. So, remember Jesus is your Lord, your loving Friend, and He is here with you. He is always with you, whether you feel it or not. Both of the sisters had a love for Jesus, but Mary carried that love at his feet, soaking in his love. Do you think she was filled with peace, with joy? Her eyes were fixed on Jesus. Nothing else mattered because her Lord was with her. The Lord loves you and He wants to have a relationship with you.

"I encourage you to do the same thing. Talk to Jesus and sit at His feet and listen to Him, and He will take away all your worries and cares. He is a loving Father and a merciful God and He wants to help you. He is reaching out to you where you are right now. He is near you. He loves you..."

Chapter 7

The Help Team

The worship service was over, and Jane drove us to the Carters' house. They were already home and a few others from the church had joined them: Patrick and Martha Reed and Sonia Peterson.

I had seen Martha and Sonia helping with food donations at church and they were almost always there, or at least when I was there.

We went into the lounge and invaded the couches, while Jim took his large armchair in a corner. Everyone was chatty and talking about the worship and the sermon, and it sounded like a room full of busy bees.

"Lovely sermon, Jim... Good things to meditate on through the week. We have so much going on, and our poor daughter Louise – it is too much for her," said Martha.

Turning toward me, Martha, a lady in her late 60s, added, "My daughter Louise is going through a divorce. She has two little kids, and Patrick and I try to help her as much as we can by going over and picking them up from school. She used to work full time, but

---

John 3:16-17

For God so loved the world, that he gave his only Son, that whoever believes in him should not perish but have eternal life. For God did not send his Son into the world to condemn the world, but in order that the world might be saved through him.

now, on top of everything, she was told that she would lose her job as they wanted someone to work every day and she can't do it." Martha looked sad.

"It is really hard for her, and we keep encouraging her to find a new job and also make new friends and come to church. She used to come when she was young. But like all of us, she had her moments and went her own way. We keep praying!" said Patrick.

Patrick was Martha's husband and older by about five years. He was a pleasant man with a kind voice.

A noise was heard and Jim stood up to open the front door. Someone else was coming. I was not sure what was going on, but it did not bother me to see so many people; it even made me feel secure and distracted me from my thoughts.

"Hello, Daniel!" Everyone was waving.

"I was wondering whether you were coming after all."

He took another armchair and joined the circle of friends.

"Yes, Sonia. My sister Katie has invited me for dinner, so I have to be there soon, otherwise she will call me all afternoon."

"How is she?" asked Margaret.

"She is fine, thank you! May was seven last week and we had to have a birthday party, and Uncle Daniel had to sing at her party. And Ella is only five." He smiled.

Everyone in the room was so much in the conversation. They seemed to be good friends and know each other's families.

I never saw Daniel except at the church, and it was a bit different to see him now at Jim's house. It was still Daniel, but I never had a chance to say more than a few words to him. This afternoon he was possibly the last person I expected to see.

Jane was concerned about me and redirected all the conversations in my direction.

"Let's look after our little Sarah as we've all gathered here today for her."

All eyes in the room turned on me. I smiled, embarrassed, and waited to hear why I was there. At work, I was capable of leading a conversation and taking decisions, but that day I was comfortable sitting on a couch, surrounded by chatty friends, and going with the flow.

Patrick spoke up.

"We are the Help Team from Grace Church! Martha, Sonia, Jane, Daniel, Margaret, Jim and me. There are a few more, but we are the team that tries to offer help to anyone who is in need."

Sonia took a cell phone from her pocket and put it on the table.

"You could say we are part of the emergency team, as well. But there is a different team for emergencies. We take turns having this phone, so if there is some need or someone is sick, we are there and we can help them. We are a team, a family."

Margaret continued, smiling.

"Prayers are important, and we back each other up with prayer. There are many intercessor teams that meet on Sunday mornings for different reasons. Confidentiality and trust are important, and also the right approach to each situation and each person, as we are all different and we face different challenges."

I was very touched and did not know how to react as I'd had quite a lot going on in my life over the past week. My mind was all over the place, and my heart started to beat faster as all eyes were turned toward me. I got lost in my thoughts, and Margaret and Jane stepped out into the kitchen and started organizing a little lunch.

Patrick, who seemed to be in charge of the Help Team, spoke up again.

"What can we do for you, Sarah?"

Daniel interrupted politely as he felt a bit lost and did not know the story.

"Can anyone please fill me in so I know what this is about?"

"Of course – I apologise. You and Sonia do not know why Sarah is here and what happen yesterday!" He looked at me. "Would you like to share your story and what happened yesterday?"

Hesitating a bit, I found my courage and spoke up.

"Yesterday, I met Jim and had a chat with him about selling my parents' house." I looked around the room and everyone was listening.

"My parents died a few years ago in a car crash and my life became work orientated. I am the manager at Creative Ideas, an advertising and fund-raising company. I was thinking that it was time for me to sell my house and have a new start in life."

I stopped and looked down, unsure whether I wanted to continue.

"Are you all right?" asked Martha.

Looking up and regaining my courage, I carried on.

"Yesterday, someone broke into my house, and at this stage, it is in a total mess, with lots of broken things everywhere. Jane, as always, looked after me and helped me pack a few things, and I slept at her house last night. You could say I've moved in with her as I cannot go back to the house."

There was silence for a minute.

Daniel looked at me and then said, "Let's lift up the matter to the Lord and ask him for wisdom and guidance. Jim, would you like to pray, please."

"Dear Heavenly Father, we bring to you Sarah and her situation. Please guide us and help us to know how to show kindness and be here for her. Give us wisdom to know your will. We thank you because you always answer our prayers. In the name of Jesus, we pray. Amen."

After a moment of silence, Martha said, "How would you like us to help you?"

"I would like to sell my house and move into a new house as a fresh start. That was my parents' house and I do not want to be stuck anymore in the past. It's time for me to move on. I've prayed and thought about it, and this is what the Lord put on my heart. What happened yesterday kind of moved things along a bit for me, even if it is a total mess."

Jane and Margaret came into the lounge with sandwiches, crackers, and salads, and it felt like a feast.

"I'm so hungry," said Daniel, looking at all the food.

"You are always hungry!" replied Jane, smiling, and patted him on the shoulder.

"Well, how are we doing at this stage?"

"We've just started."

"Let's take first things first. That house is a mess. We need to clean it and make it nice."

"Yes, Sarah?"

"Yes, Jane."

Sonia was writing things down.

"Jane and Martha, are you organizing this?"

"I will join you, too," said Margaret.

Jim asked, "What do you want to do with the things that are in the house? Are you taking them with you wherever you move?"

They all seemed to know what to do, and they'd worked together before. They were a very laid-back team and able to adapt to all kinds of situations.

"I will have to go with Jane and look at them, and I will choose a few to keep, and the rest, mostly the furniture, will be sold with the house."

"All right, if that is what you want."

Jim turned to Daniel, who was patiently listening.

"Now, over to you, boy."

Since Jim had met him a few years ago, Daniel had become for him like a son. He and Margaret were very fond of him and had looked after him for a couple of years till he got on his feet. Daniel actually spent more time with Jim than with his own father. His natural parents were in their own world, with their own friends, and kept planning to move into Abilene town but never did. They were not very interested in helping or supporting Katie or him, and in a way, they were almost strangers. Keeping contact with them was not easy as they travelled a lot and were seldom home.

Daniel was very confident and knew his place in the team.

"Maybe you know that I am looking after a company called Brick Houses. We build new houses and we also have a variety of other services, such as looking after your house and making it look better so you can sell it."

I could not believe it. It was Daniel, wasn't it? The worship leader? It was true – he was in construction! He did not look a builder type or as if he ran that kind of business, but hey, I'd learned not to be surprised anymore.

"You could look after my house, could you?"

"Yes. Firstly, I could make it nicer so you can sell it, and secondly, I could help you buy a new property or guide you to the right channels. What do you think?"

"Daniel is very good at it," said Patrick.

"Those are very good suggestions, Daniel. Yes, it would be great if I could get some help from all of you. I am a bit lost at the moment and not sure where to start."

He took a business card out of his pocket and handed it to me.

"Call me when you want things to move and when you are ready! And please do not call me early morning – after 10, please. I am never at the office before 10 am." He smiled.

"He loves his morning sleep. I keep telling Sarah not to go to the office at 8 am but cannot convince her to treasure her mornings. I would!" said Jane.

"8 am?" Daniel looked surprised.

"Yes, every morning I am there at 8 or 8:30 at the latest."

"And what time do you finish?"

"Depends – 4 or 5 pm."

Margaret defended Daniel.

"He might be at the office only at 10, but he is not usually home earlier than 6 or even 7, isn't it true, my boy?"

"Yes, it can get very late for me, and I stay extra on the work site and help the boys out."

Daniel seemed very relaxed and enjoyed talking to all of them.

Once things were established, the ladies started planning when to go to Sarah's house and what they should start with.

* * *

I started a conversation with Sarah about something other than her house.

"What did you think about the worship service this morning, Sarah?"

I was keen to hear her opinion of the singing and the new songs we'd chosen. It was not the first time I'd sung a new song, but I woke up during the night and kept practising, as if it was for an audition. Since Sarah had joined our little team, I was trying harder than before.

"It was very good, Daniel. You all did a fantastic job."

I wasn't sure whether I really believed her – she might have been being polite.

"I wish you had sung that new song with me. You have a lovely voice, Sarah."

She looked at me with her big green eyes and smiled.

"Actually, I was thinking I would like to join you guys some Sunday."

"Really? Are you serious? You won't change your mind?"

All the heads in the room turned around at my raised voice. But my friends knew me; that was Daniel.

Sarah felt embarrassed and stayed silent.

"So, you really mean it?"

"Yes, I do!"

My heart started to beat fast. I could not believe it: she would sing with me. What a joy, and I was already making plans in my head. She had such a beautiful, calm voice, and I was like a noisy, buzzy bee... ha ha!

"Next Sunday, Sarah?"

"Take it slowly, Daniel. One song next Sunday, and we will see after that how things are and how I get along!"

"Maybe two songs? Please."

She seemed unmovable. Sarah was very good with her boundaries and she did not want to get too anxious. Even one song to sing on Sunday was a challenge for her. It would take a lot of strength and courage for her to sing one song.

"No, one song and that is all, or I will not sing!"

We laughed and I backed off.

"All right! You win this time: one song!"

* * *

It was better than nothing, but the group tried to convince her to sing one more. However, she had made up her mind. It was the right timing when you felt ready, not when you were pushed to do something.

She changed more than she realized as she learned to say no. And she wanted to do things because she felt comfortable doing them, not because she was told to. It was like learning to walk again.

She was not sure what she was doing yet, but with the presence of God in her life, she got bolder and bolder, taking one step after another. The Lord was working in every area of her life, not only one. So much was going on, and even if she felt confused at times, she was seeing a bit of light and gaining wisdom and clarity.

Some boundaries were falling and new ones were getting stronger. It was as though her inner self was being rebuilt and on a new journey. It meant a lot to her that her friends were with her on this new journey, and she felt loved, accepted and optimistic.

Changing the conversation, Sarah said, "Martha, Patrick, I can give you my phone number, and if your daughter wants a job, tell her to give me a call. I have 15 hours' work for a position in one of my project teams. If she is interested!"

Everyone looked at her in surprise. They did not know much about her and her life. They loved the way she had shyly come to church with Jane. She had not been going there for a couple of years like Daniel, or for many years like Sonia. She was like a flower that had started to bloom only a few months ago.

Martha gave her a hug with tears in her eyes.

"The Lord works in all of us, through us, and His Spirit is making a way in all our lives and the lives of our loved ones. Amen!"

Daniel looked at her as they were leaving and almost whispered as she was walking to the car, "Sarah, it was very kind of you to help Martha's daughter. You still amaze me – you are full of surprises."

"Daniel, I think I am more surprised than you are as you were the last person that I expected to see today at Jim's house."

Daniel opened the car door for her. Jane was chatting with Margaret, and the others had already left. It was getting dark and cold, and Sarah started to shiver.

As she tried to wrap her coat around her, she dropped her bag, and both she and Daniel tried to catch it. He gently bumped into her, then laughed.

"I am sorry Sarah!" he said and passed the bag to her.

She felt shy and said thank you.

Before closing the car door, Daniel said, "Thank you for the one song!" She caught his eyes and kept looking at him for a moment.

Usually, she was the shy one, but this time she realized that she had a very handsome man in front of her who loved the Lord and loved music.

You had to admit that Daniel was tall and handsome and had beautiful, ocean-blue eyes.

He noticed her looking at him, then he smiled and closed the car door.

Chapter 8

Katie

It was late afternoon and Katie was already on the phone.

"Where are you, Daniel? You know little Ella is waiting for a bedtime story. You promised."

"Katie, it is not even 5 o'clock. I will be there. I just went to see Jim, and we had a little gathering of friends. I will pop to my house and then come by. I'll be there in 30 minutes. Is that all right, sis?"

Katie said something, teasing him, and hung up the phone.

When he parked his car on the driveway, he looked at his house. It was quite beautiful. He never had time to notice it. He had designed it and had it built about five years ago. A few years after his relationship with Olivia. Oh yes… what a relationship.

He still had memories of how it had all started and went so wrong. They were together for a year, and by then Katie, his sister, was already married and had kids.

Not him. His parents kept pushing him, telling him that he was already over 30 and needed to settle down. To him, settle was a bit of a joke. When he was in his 20s, he had travelled the world for two

---

Matthew 6:33-35

But seek first the kingdom of God and his righteousness, and all these things will be added to you. Therefore do not be anxious about tomorrow, for tomorrow will be anxious for itself. Sufficient for the day is its own trouble.

years with his best friend Jack. Jack was still his best friend. But he got married and his priorities and life changed. He settled down, but Daniel did not. It seemed as though things were always more complicated for him.

Olivia had been a wrong choice, and it ended up in a total mess for him. But who really cared? Only God knew what he went through.

The phone interrupted his thoughts. Oh, no, his mother again.

"Yes, Mum!"

"Katie just called and invited us for dinner. Are you coming? We haven't seen you for an awfully long time and we miss you. How are you? How are things going?"

His mother, Helen, was a lovely lady. His parents lived in a little town about three hours away from Abilene. It was just as well, otherwise she would have been at his door every day. He needed some space.

That's why he had this big house built for himself. A five-bedroom house for a single guy! He must have been crazy. Well, it was his house and he loved it.

It was 10 minutes from church, and he loved walking when he had time. And there was a big park nearby.

His thoughts were coming and going and his mum asked, "Are you listening? We are waiting for you, so keep going. See you soon."

That day, he was not in the mood to see his parents; he had seen them two or three months ago. Or to listen to their long stories about their travels. They spent more time travelling than at home. They must be feeling bored, he was thinking, or perhaps they had another idea for a date for him.

That's how he had ended up the first time in the mess with Olivia.

It had been a planned date with the daughter of a friend of a friend, and he had ended up going out with her. He'd struggled to get out of the relationship. He ended up in all sorts of things and could not even hold a job for more than a couple of months.

Well, if I could not change her, she changed me, and I ended up just drinking and partying. What an awful time... He shuddered as he remembered. *If it had not been for Patrick and Jim, who found me on the street one night...*

"Hey, you there, are you OK?"

"Let's see if he needs a doctor or a place to live. He looks like a young man, said Patrick.

"Are you all right? Do you need any help?"

He opened his eyes and saw Jim.

"Please help me. I do not want this life anymore. I need help."

"Where do you live? What is your name?"

"I am Daniel, and I no longer have a place to live. I do need some help, please, sir."

"I am Jim, and this is Patrick. We will look after you."

Jim and Margaret took him into their home and saved him from living on the streets. They looked after him and often cried with him. They became his parents, and he lived with them for almost two years.

His parents had no clue of what he was going through, and he would always find good excuses (better to call them lies) to hide the truth that he was not well. But even when he'd given up on everything, the Lord did not give up on him. In His grace and love, He found him and never let him go.

It wasn't always easy. He used to walk out in the middle of a worship service, and people looked at him. He could not settle till love found him and held him still.

He found a job in a construction company, and step by step, the Lord lead him and blessed him. The Lord carried him through the hurt and pain, but it took him several years to be able to forgive and move on with his life. Grace Church was loving and supportive and became his family.

He stopped drinking, worked hard and became a manager five years ago. The same year, the leader of the worship group retired, and he started the Eagles. It was such a blessing, and he started to find himself.

His parents were amazed at the change in their son. However, they still teased him about still being single.

Marriage was the last thing on his mind. He was determined not to follow that path and even rejected the idea of having a family. It was certainly not a priority at the moment.

When he entered the house, it was nice and clean, as if nobody lived there, and his kitchen was hardly used. There was a vast open-plan dining room and lounge, with his large TV and sound system. After work, this was where he spent most of his time, with his music. It brought him great joy and comfort.

He rushed up the stairs and felt the need for a shower, but thought it would make him late for dinner.

"Who cares?" he said aloud and went into his bedroom. It was a beautiful light blue with large windows.

He took some clothes from the wardrobe and was in and out of the shower in a flash. Maybe he was trying to get rid of certain memories, wash them away.

He was still dressing as he walked out the door and jumped into his beautiful blue BMW M5. He was late, and although he heard his phone ringing, he did not answer.

His family was a bit too much for him sometimes. He would have loved to travel and have a break from them, but at the same time, he loved them. They made his life more fun, and his two nieces were adorable.

"You're here!" his mother cried, giving him a big cuddle. She was a short lady, a bit like a teddy bear with her chestnut hair, and his father was not much taller, with a big belly and a pleasant personality. Daniel did not look like a chip off the old block. He was tall and handsome with big, beautiful, ocean-blue eyes. Nobody in the family had blue eyes, and they even wondered whether he was their son after all.

"Hello Mum, Dad, lovely to see you. After so long!" he teased them and looked at Katie. There was a resemblance between her and Daniel. She was older by two years and was a beautiful woman. He kissed her on the cheek. "Where is James? Don't tell me he's working late!"

"Yes, he is working late, again! And I had an argument with him again this morning as he is never home. We are not even a family anymore."

Turning to her mother, she continued. "The girls hardly see him; maybe on a Saturday. Now he's saying he even works weekends. I see more of Daniel and talk more with Daniel than him. I am not sure how long I can go on like this."

Two lovely angels walked into the lounge and jumped for joy.

"Uncle Daniel, Uncle Daniel, we missed you!" they squealed and cuddled him.

He took them in his arms and lifted Ella up. May said, "What about me? I might be seven, but can you lift me up too."

Daniel ran around the house playing with the girls, and his parents looked hopelessly at him.

"He will never change! It would be good for him to have a family too, and to settle down," said Michael.

"I heard that!" retorted their son.

The family sat around the dinner table, and even though his parents were not believers, Daniel said grace. His little nieces had started going to church, and he would take them with him occasionally when Katie allowed him.

She was much too busy chasing her career and trying to work over weekends. Daniel kept telling her not to, but she would not listen.

"How is work, Katie?" asked her mum.

"I am trying to get extra hours as we are struggling with money and James spends too much travelling."

Daniel was not happy with the conversation.

"There are two beautiful girls here. Can we talk about something other than money, Katie?"

Katie got angry.

"What do you know? You have your quiet life. And everything is fine for you. You don't know how hard it is for us."

Michael, a slow-moving man, smiled and tried to say a few words. "Katie, it can't be easy for you, but we are here to support you. You know we cannot give you any more money... It is very hard for us. We are planning to travel again – for our health, you know..."

Everything was for their health, but Daniel had learned over the years to love and accept his parents and was praying for them. They had their own lives and minds, and even if he did not agree with them, he had learned to respect their choices and take everything to the Lord in prayer.

"Yes, Dad. Do you know, if it had not been for Daniel, who paid some of the past months' bills, we would not have been able to stay in this house?"

She was angry and distressed, and Daniel always tried to calm her down when he was around. He needed a good night's sleep after a chat with Katie. He had suggested that she come to church and make new friends, but she knew only one thing at the moment: work, work, work.

"Oh, Daniel, how sweet and kind of you!" said his mum. She stood up and gave him a big kiss on his head.

He smiled. He knew by now to stay silent as Katie was in one of her moods and she needed someone to listen to her.

Her cell phone rang and everyone became quiet for a minute. Then the two girls started chattering. "Oh, let's tell Uncle Daniel about our new game. Nanny and Grandad brought it. Maybe he can play with us after dinner."

They smiled. Ella had beautiful, curly, chestnut hair and big green eyes, and the older one, May, was more like her father, with dark hair and hazel eyes. Daniel was so fond of them.

"Let's quickly finish dinner. We can let your mummy talk to Nanny and Grandad, and we can go and play, and I will put you to bed. What do you say?"

"And bath, Uncle Daniel. You forgot the bath!"

"Yes, we'll have some fun, but please do not splash me too much!"

Katie returned to the table looking unhappy. "I told you," she burst out. "He is not coming home tonight. Maybe on Tuesday."

Her mum said quietly, "My dear... let's talk. The girls are going to have their bath..."

Daniel understood the message and took the girls to have their bath, promising them some dessert and hot chocolate later.

"Katie, what is really going on with you and James?"

Katie left all the dishes on the table and sat down on the couch next to her dad. "James and I decided to divorce. Well... considering what is going on."

"What is going on, Katie? You never tell us anything!"

Her parents look offended, without really understanding the situation. It was not about them. It was about Katie and her family.

Crying, she said through her hiccups, "He is having an affair and told me he's leaving me for her. And ... she is even pregnant."

Her mum almost fainted. "What?!" she cried.

"OK, calm down, Helen. Let's see what is going on and how we can help her."

"You can't help me," said Katie. "It is all over, and that's that. I am not sure how I will even pay for the divorce or what I will do... I am totally lost."

Daniel heard her as he came into the room. "Uncle Daniel will pay for it, and you are moving in with me, as long as I can still have two rooms. You can have three rooms. Hey, Katie."

He went to her, wiped her tears and gave her a cuddle. "Little brother to the rescue."

It was as though her parents were not there. They never did much, anyway, and were not sure how to handle things like that.

But Katie started crying even more, covering her face with her hands.

"Katie, we are here to help you too," said her dad. "Helen, I had better go and listen to a bedtime story with Daniel; this is too much for me... You girls have your talk."

He kissed his daughter and went with Daniel to the next room. It was a lot for Helen and Michael to process; it was all so unexpected.

Daniel seemed to be the one on his feet. He already knew what was going on but had promised Katie he would say nothing about it. He had seen how James treated her when he was home; Daniel often had to calm him down as he was very abusive.

How had Katie ended up in this mess? James had been her sweetheart from university. They broke up, but he resurfaced seven years later... with nothing. He found Katie, and she had been in this situation for several years. She never wanted to admit it, but Daniel was a patient man and he was always there for her. Some things, however, are not good and they need to end.

His heart went out to his sister and he was there almost daily with her. The best idea was for her to move in with him as it was becoming too much for him to be all over the place – work, church, Katie – and he did not want to crash again. The Lord had taught him over the years to say no if things became overwhelming. He had learnt to seek His face and prioritise what was important and best in his life.

It had taken him years to learn to invite the Lord into everything, into his day-to-day life. He not only prayed but talked to the Lord and sang to the Lord, at work, driving, in church, wherever he was. The Lord was everything to him.

Chapter 9

Changing

It was already morning and the start of another week. Daniel was finally up. He had not heard the first two alarms but managed to hear the third one, and by then it was 8.45. He jumped out of bed and flew around the house.

Drinking his coffee, he took his Bible and spent 20 minutes reading and in meditation and prayer. In his house, worship music played almost all the time, creating quite an atmosphere.

His phone was already was buzzing and he had five messages. By 9.45 he was driving to work. He parked in front of an interesting building with three levels. It was geometrically designed, with red patterns and beautiful triangular and rectangular windows. As he entered, his secretary spoke before he'd even said good morning.

"Sir, you already have the window company on hold; shall I put them through?"

"Good morning, Becky. No, tell them I will call back. Just let me get into my office. If I was an angel and could fly, it might accelerate things." He smiled.

Joshua 1:8

This Book of the Law shall not depart from your mouth, but you shall meditate on it day and night, so that you may be careful to do according to all that is written in it. For then you will make your way prosperous, and then you will have good success.

"Now, let's start at the beginning and take it one step at a time. Let's see what is going on today and decide how to plan it. You should know that by now, Becky; you've worked here for more than two years."

Becky was a pleasant, old-fashioned lady in her late 50s and went to a Baptist church. She was a dedicated secretary and became anxious if Daniel was late for anything, but she had discovered that Daniel had his own way of doing things. She had lived alone all her life and had been rather isolated.

Daniel passed a few offices and said hello. Everyone was already busy. Many worked 9 to 5 and some were part-time. His favourite part of the day was when he had to organize deliveries of material and was able to work a bit with the "boys" as he called them. The builders never understood why a manager would like to get his hands dirty and not even be paid for it, but they admired him and loved it when he was there with them.

But Daniel's standards were not the same as everyone else's. Through his relationship with the Lord, his life had changed from living for himself and what he wanted to being able to identify what was needed in his life and what the Lord wanted to give him. He was living a life of grace, giving, serving and always being available – wherever the Lord called him. It was not always easy, but he found joy and delight in what he was doing, and time and space did not matter.

He loved his church and the music; he loved being there. His life became fulfilled and peaceful on the one hand, yet he was always amazed at how each day was full of surprises that he would have to deal with one by one and yes, prioritise. Not only at work, but at church and in his new role of looking after his sister and his lovely two nieces.

"Becky, please come to my office. Bring the diary and let's start!"

Becky, with her white hair and black dress, came into the office with her pen poised to write. Daniel looked very relaxed in dark blue trousers and an open-neck shirt. He'd never liked ties, but he loved his shoes. However, he always had a change of clothes in his office and a pair of trainers for when he went to a work site and spent time with the boys.

His blue eyes sparkled as he looked at the big pile of papers in front of him. He was very organized, but at the same time, there were files all over the place. He had his own system and nobody was allowed to touch it.

"Let's look at the deliveries for today. Hmm... yes... yes." He read through the list of things he had to sort out.

"Get me the window company, and also I need to talk to Supply Go. They're supposed to deliver the materials I ordered today. I have to leave after lunch for the flat site. And yes..." He looked at her, thinking.

Becky was very quiet, writing and waiting.

"Yes, contact the real estate agency for me. I need to talk to Mark and see what else... Yes, the house that we started to build last week. Contact the boys; I need to speak to them. That's all. Give me 10 minutes and then start the phone calls. I have so much to sort out!"

He stood up and was in such a good mood. He looked taller than usual. He stretched and looked at the pile of papers. As he took one of them, the phone started ringing.

"Mr. Anderson, your sister wants to talk to you. She seems distressed."

Daniel was not expecting to deal with Katie that morning. He'd just spent his whole evening listening to the same stories again and again and nothing seemed to change.

"Yes, Katie is a priority, anytime she calls, Becky. I forgot to tell you. Pass her over."

Katie at the other end of the phone was crying.

"Daniel, I cannot do this anymore. He keeps trying to call me and argue with me and threatens me... I cannot live like this."

Daniel took a big deep breath; finally, after five minutes, he said, "Katie, let's meet for lunch and discuss what to do. Come to my office and we'll eat at the canteen. We will see what can be done. Let me pray and think about it and also do some work. Yes, Katie, Please remember I have lots of people depending on me and I need to work."

Katie felt bad.

"Oh, Daniel, I do not know what I would do without you. You are always here for me and always helping me, and oh, my, what a wonderful brother you are..."

Daniel interrupted her as his other phone was ringing.

"Katie, I have to go. I have an incoming call. I will see you here at 1.00. OK... and please calm down. I have only one hour free. Try not to talk for more than an hour," he teased her.

His heart was deeply troubled by what his sister was going through and he wished he could help her more. Divorce was not fun. James was not interested in his girls, sadly; he did not even want to see them. His idea of being a dad was seeing them once a month. And that is what he was asking from Katie through the solicitors, but he did want half the house. It always came down to money for some people.

All morning, there were phone calls, and his office door was always open. People were coming and going and bringing or taking files. He had a table with two stacks: one for documents to be taken and another for documents to be left for him to look at.

"Daniel, did you look at the A2 file report"? asked a young man. "I need to send it today."

Daniel looked up. "Yes, Nick, it is done. You did a great job. Fantastic presentation and good deals and ideas!" He smiled.

The boy was so excited. He was in his early 20s and enjoyed working at Brick Houses.

"Thank you! I was not sure whether I'd managed it better this time. You corrected it quite a lot for me last week!"

"No, this time, you got it. Keep going, keep going. Do not forget to send it off, and let me know what they say about it. We need good deals so we can move on." He handed him a file with lots of numbers and a graphic presentation.

The young man smiled. "Of course, sir, I will send it straight away!"

"Nick, come by in the morning; I might have some extra work for you."

"Oh, really? Thank you. That would be great. What time – 9 o'clock?"

"Nick, you know I don't arrive till 10.00, and you know I also have my morning busy time with phone calls and a lot of other stuff... yes!"

"Of course Daniel, I forgot; got a bit carried away."

Daniel left his office, and as he was going to the canteen, he said hello to Maria. She was a very good chef and a lovely lady with five children. Her husband worked for the company as a builder. They attended Grace Church, and Daniel had got her husband a job a few years ago.

"Daniel, how are you today?"

"Doing great, Maria! What is for lunch?" He smelled the food and saw a range of trays from which he could choose.

"You know our usual multi selection!"

"Yes, yes... I know. It is always so delicious. Feeding hundreds of people is quite a challenge, isn't it? But you are doing such a good job. And so are your four little helpers, the lovely young girls who seem to be learning lots of things from you."

She chuckled. She was a petite Chinese lady and spoke very fast English. All her children were grown up, and she loved cooking and looking after people. She was part of a cooking team at church that made Saturday food deliveries to less fortunate neighbourhoods.

"Oh, Maria, Katie is coming today. She does not eat a lot, but please put her down on the registry as a guest."

"Of course, Mr. Anderson, we shall do that."

As he sat down with his big selection of food, from hot soup to cold meats and salads, Katie sat down next to him.

It was not the first time she had been there, and she went and made her little food selection on a tray. She returned looking sad.

"Let's pray, Katie!"

"Of course, Daniel. You and your prayers."

"Dear Lord, our Father, we thank you for such a blessed time and thank you for Katie, that she is here. Thank you for the food that Maria and her team cooked. We ask for your wisdom and guidance and your Spirit so we can see what your will is in Katie's situation. We ask for peace and healing for this broken family. In the name of Jesus, we pray. Amen."

"Why do you always pray?"

Daniel smiled as he liked to be asked about the Lord and how wonderfully God was working in his life.

"Because prayer is a way to connect with the Lord, our Father. It's a way of communication and seeking God's will. God wants a relationship with us and wants us to ask Him for His help and to be part of our lives. Life with Jesus is much easier, Katie. I wish you would come to church and see what I am talking about."

Katie looked at him, amazed.

"You know, considering what a mess you were when you were younger and all that you went through with Mum and Dad bossing you around, you've really changed. You've had all kinds of hard times, a broken relationship and travelling all over the place. Now look at you – a manager. Who would have thought that? And at church, singing worship music and on the Help Team. Helping me!"

Daniel looked at his sister. Yes, she was right, he had changed.

"Now, Katie... without tears, please... I want to know what is going on! And please give me the short version. The boys will be waiting for me after lunch." He laughed.

"Of course, Daniel. My solicitor is sorting out the documents and I need to pay her. That is the first problem, and it is quite a lot. And I am broke, as you know. Secondly, I cannot be in the house when James comes back this week. I need to go somewhere with the girls. We keep arguing... I still have work, and it is not easy and not good for the girls, either."

Daniel was impressed with how quickly she finished talking.

"All right, sis. Fine, I will help you with the solicitor. Give me the bill and I will pay it for you. So that's one thing you do not need to worry about."

Katie touched his hand and with tears in her eyes said, "I am the big sister, and I should look after you, and here you are, my little brother, looking after me and my mess. I promise I will pay you back..."

"No, I do not want you to pay me back... I want you to start looking after yourself and the girls. Forget James, and together we will move on. I am here for you, in the best way I can be, Katie. I wish you did not have to go through this."

"Thank you, Daniel."

"Now, secondly, you can move into my house today. Pack some things and you can move in with me. You can have three rooms, you and my lovely sweet nieces, and I will keep two rooms, if that is OK with you."

She jumped off the chair and hugged her brother, which was a bit embarrassing as a lot of people were at lunch.

"You know what? I will do something for you, Daniel. I will come to church on Sunday with the girls. You said there are some groups for kids, and they could go there and I could see you singing. I heard you are quite good."

"You should come to church for God, not for me, Katie."

Daniel was not sure what he was doing, but he just moved his sister and his nieces in with him. Maybe sooner than he had planned. He did like his private time and he was not sure how would adapt to the new noisy house and extra little feet bouncing around.

"Katie, I will contact the Help Team and ask some of them to come and help you pack. You already know Margaret and Jim and Jane. There is a van that can bring your things over to my house, so that will all be sorted out. Then you can sort out the unpacking as and when you have time. We will have to let the solicitors know that you are moving with me as it is unbearable for you. Are you sure you can handle it, by yourself?"

"Yes, Daniel, it would be good to let the solicitors know as they already know about the situation. And it's a brilliant idea to ask Grace Church to help me."

Before she'd finished, Daniel was on the phone, speaking to Patrick, and things were organised. Martha and Margaret and, of course, Jane said yes, and Daniel asked them to be at Katie's house at 4 pm.

What an amazing Lord who guides and provides. He helps us and works in us and through us and brings us all together as a family to look after each other.

Chapter 10

Broken heart – heal me, Lord

The Lord is always good; the Lord always comes to the rescue.

It was late, 11 pm, and the girls were asleep. Katie had managed to move all her things far more quickly than she had expected.

"Thank you, Daniel... and thank you, ladies!"

"We have to go home now, Katie. Look after yourself, and we will pray for you. You are a lovely young lady, and Daniel will look after you. He is a good brother, isn't he?" added Margaret.

She looked at him and said from the bottom of her heart, "He is the best brother I could ever wish for! I do not know what I would have done without him."

As she left, Margaret gave him a hug and whispered, "You are doing something amazing, Daniel. Jim and I and the church are very proud of you."

Daniel was tired after his unexpectedly full day. He asked Katie to be so kind as to talk to their parents the next day as he had a busy schedule ahead and had to catch up with his personal life.

John 14:6

Jesus said to him, "I am the way, and the truth, and the life. No one comes to the Father except through me. If you had known me, you would have known my Father also. From now on you do know him and have seen him."

It was midnight by the time he went to bed, and he could not sleep. The next day was Friday, and the week was already gone. His mind was still flying all over the place, and one of the images that popped up was Sarah.

He had promised to help her with searching for a new house. He had given her his phone number, and it was up to her to call him. He was wondering whether she would. He could hear the small, kind voice in his heart, the Holy Spirit prompting him to pray for Sarah. He had prayed before for her, but this time, he was not sure how to pray.

As he started praying, all kinds of ideas came into his mind. Following the guidance of the Holy Spirit, he prayed about issues from helping her buy a new house to singing with her on Sunday.

For the first time in a long time, he thought about why he'd had such a big house built for himself. Yes, he had hoped for a family of his own one day, but as time passed, he forgot about it and even stopped praying for it. He found the hardest person to pray for was himself. Only the Lord knew the desires of his heart. He, for sure, did not know what he wanted in life. Well, yes, a great job, a great house, amazing friends... what else could he have wanted? Others wanted things, but he didn't.

Sometimes his heart would get lonely and he would miss having someone in his life – the sweet romance and flowers and dating – but he had been so broken after his first relationship that he did not want to risk it again.

However, he did think of Sarah a few times and she seemed a very nice lady. What was her story? He knew only a few bits and bobs from Jane and what she'd shared regarding her parents.

She was not in a relationship, was she?

Why would he think of that? That was a very good question!

He turned over, watched the stars through the curtains and slowly drifted off.

Friday morning was cold and he was not in the mood for office work and phone calls. He wanted to go and work on the site, but Becky kept reminding him of last-minute things that needed to be sorted out so she could send some emails.

His mind was flying around and he was thinking about what he would do over the weekend.

"Do I need to repeat it, sir!?" asked Becky, waking him up.

"No, it's fine, thank you, Becky. I will sort it out for you within an hour and you can email the information across."

Then Nick knocked at the opened door.

"May I come in?"

"Yes, I'm almost finished. Would you please check those figures? I think I am missing one and I have run out of time!"

"No problem, sir. And shall I pass them to Becky!"

"Yes, please. Thank you, Nick."

Daniel took his coat and prepared to leave.

"I'll be on a work site, at the flats. Anything comes up, call me."

In the car, the worship songs were very bouncy, but he chose to listen to a very quiet CD.

The moment he arrived at the work site, his phone rang.

What is the matter now? Can I not have 30 minutes to myself! he thought.

"Hello Daniel, This is Becky. You've just received a phone call from a lady called Sarah Grant. She left her phone number if you want to give her a call when you have time. I told her you were out..."

Sarah, Sarah... He could not think for a minute. *Oh yes, Sarah. Of course – what was I thinking?*

"Yes, please give me her phone number."

What a surprise, to receive a phone call from her. They were due to meet the next day for their Saturday morning worship practice.

He was not sure whether to call her. Maybe later. It made him anxious, not knowing what to say to her. He'd had a busy week and felt tired and did not want to gather his thoughts for a conversation.

The day passed quickly and it was almost 6 pm when he remembered that he had not returned her call.

He picked up his phone and called her, without planning what to say.

"Hello Sarah, I am returning your call. I know it is a bit late. So sorry, but I've been very busy!"

"No problem. Thank you for getting back to me. I was wondering whether you could help me regarding my house... you know." She was speaking rather slowly and it sounded like a whisper.

"Yes, when is best for you? You could pop into my office and we can see what we can do for you?"

"We meet tomorrow, don't we? It is Saturday!"

"Oh, it is Saturday. So I will see you tomorrow!"

The time passed quickly and Daniel was the last one to leave. When he got home, Katie was already putting the girls to bed.

"You are late, again. Do you know it is 7.30?"

"Katie, please, you know I work from 10 am and often work until 7."

Katie shook her head and left him. She realized her brother was working hard and learned to respect him. She started cooking for him late and felt that was the least she could do, considering all the evenings he even put the girls to bed after coming from work.

He sat on the couch, took his guitar and started to play a song. His nieces heard it and came to join him. However, it sounded a bit sad and they asked for a happy song. Daniel warmed up the room with a lovely, joyful song.

The girls started dancing in their pyjamas and laughing, and Katie joined in too.

"It's good to see you laugh, Katie!"

"Let's go to bed, girls. Uncle Daniel needs to have a shower and dinner, yes?"

Daniel was lost in his thoughts. He started playing his guitar again, a soft song with no words, and he kept playing for quite a while. He smiled and ran his hands through his hair. *Hmm... worship practice tomorrow. Something to look forward to or maybe not?*

He couldn't sleep till late and decided to look through his music for some new worship songs. He went into his room, and it must have been after 1 am by the time he finally went to bed.

A thought crossed his mind: if he did not wake up in the morning, what would happen to Katie, the worship group and his team of "boys" from Brick Houses? He smiled and whispered, *The Lord will look after them and raise up another Daniel, possibly much better than me. The Lord never leaves us, and he always finds a way to reach all of us. His grace, His grace is always there for us, and we are so blessed. So if tomorrow never comes, there is still a tomorrow!*

A few hours later, he heard a knock on the door.

"Daniel, are you asleep?"

"Are you all right, Katie?" He jumped out of bed, not even knowing where he was, and opened the door.

"Katie, can you not sleep again? Would you like me to make you some tea?"

They went downstairs and Daniel looked at his sister.

"Katie, you need to sleep. It's 4 o'clock and it will be morning soon."

She looked sad and smiled.

"How long can I stay here, Daniel?"

"I've already told you: as much as it takes and as long as you need. Please don't ask me again. You know I try my best to keep my word. Look, I have an idea." He stood up from the couch, took his guitar and started playing again.

"You play so beautifully and ... you are so good to us. I will never be able to repay you."

"Listen, Katie... let's send the girls somewhere tomorrow. I will call Jane. I am sure she and the ladies from the Help Team will be happy to take your beautiful angels away for a few hours, and you will have some time for yourself. What do you think? And you and I... we will go to my worship practice at church and then I'll take you for lunch. I am meeting Jack, remember. My best friend."

Katie was not sure and started indicating no with her hands.

"Listen, it is done. I will sort things out tomorrow morning. We need to get you out of the house, and you need to learn to look after yourself again."

He gave her a kiss on the cheek and said, "I'm going back to bed, and you too, and we can get some sleep tonight." He walked back to his bedroom, taking his guitar with him.

He started to think about Sarah again. She had big green eyes and she always got shy. She seemed to enjoy singing with the Eagles. And this coming Sunday, she'd promised that she would sing a song with him. Wow. That would be great. The entire church would be able to welcome her as part of the Eagles.

He could not fall asleep, so he prayed and then played his guitar till late.

Chapter 11

Hannah

Today was the day – Saturday! A day full of activities and events, one after another.

Daniel was ready when the doorbell rang, and there was Jane.

"Hello, handsome boy!" She gave him a hug, and he smiled and showed her in. She was looking forward to taking the girls out and spending time with them. She started telling Daniel all her plans but his thoughts were elsewhere.

"Daniel, are you here?"

Feeling he'd been caught, he said, "Not really. I have worship practice and for once, I would like to be on time... or try to make it on time!"

"Yes, yes... I will sort things out with Katie. You run along."

Daniel looked in the mirror. *Who are you really, Daniel?* That was a good question. For a moment he stayed looking at his reflection, and yes, he looked good in his beautiful, dark red t-shirt and a pair of blue jeans. He picked up his guitar. He had a few of them, but he had a deep connection with this one and he took it everywhere.

He smiled to himself. *Let's sing, boy!*

He managed to be late – only 10 minutes, which was impressive. The band was practising while they waited for him. Mark had sung a few songs, and Ruth was practising a song that she had chosen.

He walked in quickly, looking for someone, and felt a bit disappointed. Sarah was not there. Well, he was there for the music, and it was up to her whether she would show up or not. However, she had promised to sing this Sunday.

"Hey Daniel, you are almost on time!" said Mark.

"Can you believe it? For once he might not be late!"

Daniel said hello to everyone, took his jacket off and started singing straight away, which surprised the band.

He closed his eyes and was flying with the song, and when he opened his eyes, Sarah was in front of the stage looking at him. He felt strange and backed up a few steps on the stage. He suddenly stopped in the middle of the song while the band was still singing. Sarah started singing as she walked onto the stage, and then he joined her.

It shocked him the way she'd popped up in front of him. He had been so deep into the song that he got a fright. She was the last thing he'd expected to see.

"You came!"

"Yes. I did promise." She smiled.

Katie was there and Daniel was happy to see his sister. She was touched by her brother's singing. He was so good. His passion for music was so deep and obvious in the way he was acting; every part of his body was singing.

Margaret was there and keeping an eye on Katie.

Daniel had not seen his sister smiling for a long time, and stray tears were running down her cheeks. He jumped off the stage and gave her a big hug. He could have taken the stairs, but Daniel had his own style of doing things. He held her tight and whispered, "I really love you, Katie. You are the sweetest, best sister I have!"

His friends were not surprised as he was all over the place when he was singing; when he bounced on and off the stage, they just kept going. Sarah was getting used to his bouncy moods and found them surprising but good.

The music went on and on for more than an hour. Sarah had great fun and joined them in most of the songs.

"Sarah, are you still singing with me in only one song tomorrow?"

"Yes, of course; just one for now."

"I don't mind singing!" said a bold voice nearby. Daniel recognised a very old friend, Hannah. He used to sing with her a long time ago.

"Hannah, you're here! I heard you were abroad, and now... back here?"

"Yes, I came back for a few months, but I'll return to New York in February as I have a contract there. For now, I am here!"

Daniel and his friends were very happy to see Hannah. She had been part of the worship team for a couple of months, and she was good. She was a beautiful young lady with a remarkable career in New York as an artist and graphic designer.

She gave them all a hug, then looked curiously at Sarah.

"I am Hannah; nice to meet you."

After shaking hands with her, she moved on and looked at her old friends.

"Shall we sing, boys?" she said, laughing.

Her brown eyes were beautiful. With a lovely big smile, she took Daniel by the hand and said confidently, "May I sing?"

She took over the stage, and she had great fun jumping around. The room soon filled with all kinds of people coming from all sides of the church. It felt like a Sunday.

Sarah stepped down silently, feeling a bit embarrassed; she was not like this bouncing girl. Daniel was singing beautifully with her. She could play with her voice, stop and start again, and use all kinds of techniques. Girls like that always intimidated Sarah, and she wanted to leave.

She said goodbye to Margaret and Katie and walked towards the exit.

Daniel jumped down and ran after her. She stopped in surprise.

"Sarah, please do not go!" he said, touching her shoulder gently.

"It's OK; you need to catch up with Hannah. You all seem to be friends and I am busy. It was nice to sing with you guys. Please say goodbye for me." She smiled a little sadly and walked away.

"Are you singing with me tomorrow – please?"

She turned her head and looked at him. "Not sure. You have Hannah, and she is much better than me. I am just 'me' – singing and enjoying being with you guys and with you..."

He didn't know what to say. Jim had heard part of the conversation and whispered to Daniel, "Let it go now; let it go."

Daniel looked puzzled. "Why, Jim? Why won't she sing with me now? I so wanted to sing with her."

"Shh, boy, you can be really slow sometimes. Hannah just came..."

Daniel turned and looked at the stage, and then it got it to him. Yes, Hannah, with her impulsive attitude and confidence, might have scared Sarah.

He did not want to give up, so he ignored Jim and ran toward the main entrance. Sarah had already left the building, and he saw a car leaving. He jumped in front of the car and put his hands on the bonnet. Sarah got a fright and braked hard.

He got into the car next to her. "I am sorry, but I can't let you go." His voice was soft and he put his hand on her hand.

"Listen, Hannah is an old friend and was part of the worship group some years ago. She lives in New York and just came home for a while."

Sarah was looking straight and said nothing.

"Please say something."

"What would you like me to say?" She turned toward him.

"Anything!"

"I am not sure I am ready to sing on Sunday. It is too much for me." She looked away sadly.

"You promised, Sarah and… I chose that song just for you to sing with me. I can't believe it. Do as you please." He got out of the car, shut the door and left without looking back.

She drove off and kept her word on Sunday; she did not sing with him at all. On the other hand, Hannah sang three songs with him and she was good. She seemed to be very popular and had a lot of fun.

All the band members said hello to Sarah, and she talked to Maria as they planned to go for lunch after the service.

"Sarah, I will talk to you in a minute. Let me catch up with Hannah a bit as I might meet with the band and her later in the week."

"No problem. I can meet you at Rosie's at 1.00. Would that be OK?"

"How are you Sarah?" asked Thomas.

"We missed singing with you!"

Hannah, who was chatting with Daniel and Ruth, turned around. "Oh, so sorry, darling. I didn't know I spoiled your singing. Would have been nice to hear you sing. Daniel and the boys are so good. And Ruth and I are pretty good together as well. Are we not?!"

Daniel was not even looking at her and was not happy with her at all.

"It's OK. I am not quite part of the Sunday team. I just come to Saturday practice."

"Daniel, tell her to sing with us…"

"No, I won't. It's her choice whether she sings or not. Hey Hannah, boys, let's go for lunch."

Sarah just smiled and caught Daniel's direct gaze. It was so cold she felt rejected.

Huh… you are in trouble. Daniel is not happy with you. You'd better see what you are doing, girl.

The week passed and Daniel did not call her to organize a meeting regarding her house. Sarah kept wondering whether would be a good idea to call him.

She also prayed about the situation but did not hear a yes to singing again with the band or Daniel. It is true she felt put off by Hannah and her attitude, and she was not the kind of person to be pushy or chatty... She was Sarah! She was who she was, and in her journey, she was learning to know herself, but she still had a long way to go.

She could not be who she was not. She was a shy and sweet young woman with a broken heart that was healing. She wanted to move on with her life, but it was not easy.

On Saturday, she wanted so much to go to church and sing, but she could not. She knew Daniel was upset with her, and she did not know what to say or how to face him. She had not kept her word and he was right to be angry. She gave Margaret a nice excuse and hid and cried for a couple of hours.

On Sunday, during worship service, Daniel glanced at her once or twice but she lowered her eyes in embarrassment. Margaret noticed and after the service drew her aside. "Sarah, you did not come yesterday for worship practice. I know you are not singing on Sundays, but I thought that you loved singing. Is something going on between you and Daniel? I know it's not my place to speak, but Daniel is like a son to Jim and me, and we would like to help. Would you like me to pray for anything?"

"I need prayers, for sure. Can we talk somewhere private?" She looked around and Margaret showed her a quiet little study room. Sarah sat down on the couch and began with a heavy heart. "Margaret, I am..." She stopped and tried again.

"I love singing. I loved Saturdays. However, I am not like Daniel or the others... I'm not like Mark or Hannah. I am me."

Seeing that Margaret was listening, she carried on. "I am a very shy person, OK? I might be good at my work, but that's different. Dealing with people is hard for me sometimes as I am a very private person."

"OK, Sarah. But you are a sweet, adorable young lady with a beautiful character!"

"Daniel is upset with me as I promised a few weeks ago that I would sing one song with him on Sunday. Then I backed off when Hannah came and sang. He hasn't spoken to me since, just hi and goodbye. I couldn't come on Saturday as I felt I wasn't needed anymore."

"We'll sort it out for you. First, you should come on Saturday. Not for the team, for Daniel. Just you and the Lord. Think about it. Then it would have been good to talk to Daniel as you promised to sing with him. I would have been upset too."

Looking at her and smiling, Margaret said, "You are a lovely young lady. We are all so different and the Lord loves each of us the way we are. You are special, loved. Be who you are. Just do not give up if Hannah, or Daniel or Mark or Maria or someone else, sings or dances or even is better than you. You be best for the Lord and be yourself."

"What about Daniel? I do not want him to be upset with me. I love singing with the Eagles and with him."

"Talk to him and explain it to him. I am sure he will understand. But before you do anything, pray and wait for the Lord to guide you. When you are ready, join the Saturday group again and also pray about singing on Sundays. See what the Lord says. Learn to listen and trust when the Lord prompts you. Even if is hard, Sarah. He loves you."

Chapter 12

Meeting Daniel

It was Monday morning and Sarah took Margaret's advice. She prayed and waited for the Lord. On Friday, she heard the Lord speaking to her heart about meeting Daniel, and she followed the prompting of the Spirit and called him.

"Hello, may I speak to Daniel Anderson, please?"

"Yes, just a moment, please."

Daniel heard Becky saying, "A Miss Sarah Grant is calling you. Shall I pass the call, sir?"

He was not sure why she wanted to call. She had upset him so much, after all his hard work searching for songs he could sing with her. She could not sing even one. She had just walked away and now even dropped the Saturday worship practice.

Hannah had sung with them the past two Sundays and was pretty good, but he was not happy with her. He had spoken to Jim about it. She had arrived out of the blue, and it did not seem right for her to just jump in and join the Eagles. They were a team following the Spirit, dedicated in prayer and in a bond of friendship with each other. Hannah's attitude was not right, but Jim had told him to give her a chance, so he did.

Daniel remembered Becky's voice asking him about the phone call.

"Hello, Daniel speaking."

"Hello, Daniel. This is Sarah, Sarah Grant. I was wondering whether I could meet you for a coffee, today if you have time."

"All right, Sarah, I will make some time for you. I will meet you in an hour at Rosie's."

"Thank you. I'll see you there."

He was not sure why he'd agreed to meet her. Maybe he was curious to see what she wanted or whether she would give him 101 reasons why she could not sing.

It was good to go to Rosie's on a sunny day and have a lovely meal outside.

Daniel was well-known there as the band would often go there. They had their own table reserved on weekends.

Sarah was a bit late, and he was already seated at a little round table. He was wearing his black shirt with an open collar, and his hair was a bit messy. He had ordered a drink and was waiting patiently, looking at his watch.

She walked in, dressed in her office clothes: black trousers and a beautiful dark pink shirt. The waiter took her to his table, and he stood up politely as she sat down.

Usually, Daniel would be very chatty, but this time he just studied her, waiting for her to speak first. She had asked for this meeting, after all. Her eyes looked beautiful and kind. Her face betrayed some concern, but he pretended not to notice and smiled a little. The moment he saw her, he forgot that he was upset with her.

"Hello Daniel, again, and thank you for coming."

"Hello, Sarah."

She ordered a drink, looked around at all the other people, then looked at him. He was waiting for her to speak.

"Well, Daniel, I prayed and the Lord wanted me to come and talk to you."

This is a good start, thought Daniel.

"I am listening."

"I, I came here because I... er..." She looked down. She always found it difficult to start conversations which caused her anxiety. And meeting Daniel was quite emotional for her.

He realized was it was hard for her to start talking, and he softened his heart.

"You came here to talk me, Sarah."

She raised her head and looked into his eyes.

"Yes, I came to say I am sorry. I promised to sing with you on Sunday and I did not keep my promise. I am sorry."

"No, you didn't keep your promise, Sarah. And you upset me. You even made me angry in the car park. And you know I do not often get angry."

She took a deep breath and shook her head.

"I am just a very private person – shy! I find it difficult in some situations. At work, I'm a manager and I find it easier to deal with things. When Hannah came to church, I felt I could not sing and I was no longer needed in the band. Margaret looked after me and spoke to me. I realised I had the wrong approach to singing. She explained to me about worshipping the Lord the way I am and not worrying if I am not the best at singing. Many things like this. She encouraged me to pray and to speak to you."

"Of course, my lovely Margaret."

Looking at him, she almost whispered, "Could I come again on Saturdays, please? Even though I am not like Maria or you or even Hannah. I am me. So please be patient with me. I promise I won't run away again." Her eyes were brimming with tears.

Daniel smiled. "What am I going to do with you?" He took a deep breath.

"Please, Daniel, talk to the Eagles. I would love to sing."

"You know, Sarah, it took me three hours to find the song Surrender, and I was so looking forward to singing it with you. You have a beautiful, gentle voice. You are very gifted, and I felt so honoured to sing with you. When you just left, I felt disappointed and even hurt. What you're doing today must be very hard for you, and I treasure it. Thank you."

He put one hand on his heart and gently stretched out the other to take her hand.

"Of course you can come back. It was not the same without you."

She wanted to withdraw her hand from his but did not. Their eyes met, and for a moment, it was quiet enough to hear their heartbeats.

Her hand was cold and small and delicate.

When the lunch came, he was still holding her hand.

"Can you let go of my hand?" she said.

"Oh sorry, I forgot!" He laughed.

They had a lovely time and Daniel shared many things with Sarah. He told her that Katie with her two beautiful daughters, May and Ella, had moved in.

"You should come for dinner sometime. My nieces are adorable. And I would love to show you my research into new songs." He was not upset with her anymore and was very chatty and full of energy. He didn't seem to want to stop.

"Daniel, I also need to talk to you about my house."

Daniel paused and looked shocked. "I forgot about your house! Of course. You will need to come to my office. We definitely need to meet again."

"Yes... when I have time."

She looked at him very gratefully, and he stopped for a moment. "Are you all right, Sarah?"

She had tears on her cheeks and wanted to stand up and leave.

"You are always so kind to me and I do not deserve it. Thank you. Maybe I had better go."

He gently put his hand on her arm.

"Please, Sarah, do not run away again! Stay. I am the one thankful that you talked to me. I am sorry I was not patient enough with you and did not try to understand you better."

He took a handkerchief from his pocket and gave it to her. She wiped her tears and looked at him with wide eyes.

"Why are you extra nice to me?"

"Because you are adorable!" he replied without hesitation.

As they were leaving, he said, "You need to make time for me, please! I'll see you tomorrow, Sarah. We can talk then about your house."

"Yes, tomorrow. Goodbye."

Sarah did show up on Saturday, and Margaret whispered, "I am very proud of you!"

She was wearing a pair of blue jeans and a white T-shirt, very different from her normal work clothes, and she'd let down her shoulder-length hair. Before coming, she'd had a long chat with the Lord and asked the Holy Spirit to help her. Once she had finished praying, she felt peaceful and ready. She was not sure what she was ready for, but the Lord would lead the way.

Daniel was already there, which was unusual, as he was generally late on Saturdays and the band started practising without him. Sarah did not know that Daniel had spent hours during the night practising all kinds of songs and exploring new releases.

Daniel was dressed in his dark blue jeans and his lovely light blue t-shirt. He looked pretty good, with his hair a bit messy. That was Daniel.

When he saw her, he smiled but did not stop singing. For him, being on stage was exciting and he loved it. It filled him with joy, and he loved to inspire others.

As Sarah sat down in the front row, Hannah whooshed onto the stage and waved to everyone. Daniel raised his hand and the band immediately stopped.

Daniel said, in a very firm voice, "Hannah, it's good to see you here. However, I would prefer it if you didn't jump on the scene so much when you come. This is worship practice. You are not part of this band at the moment. We did let you sing the last two Sundays as you sang here long ago. Now, today we're practising, and certain things are in place and to be respected regarding our worship at Grace Church. Do you think you could ask before you jump on the stage?"

Hannah pushed him gently with her hand. "You really think you are the boss? Forget it, you are not so good after all. I sing with bigger people than you." She left the stage and walked away.

Daniel said nothing but his eyes met Jim's and he got his approval. He was not the type to put people in their place, but when someone did not understand a situation, you had to step in and take action.

He knew he'd done the right thing and went back to the song.

Sarah observed it all and was surprised by his reaction and that the band agreed with it. He lead with a gentle touch. He raised his hand and the band continued. Then he took his microphone and started singing the song Surrender.

He moved toward the front of the stage and smiled at Sarah. He stretched out his hand and she walked up the stairs. He took her hand and guided her to a microphone, and she started singing with him. She was smiling her beautiful smile, and for the first time in a long time, she enjoyed herself singing. Their eyes met and they both were flying with the song. She was good.

When the song was over, everyone was happy.

"Well done, Sarah," said Thomas.

Daniel laughed and pushed for more.

"Shall we sing it again?"

She looked into his eyes and smiled.

"All right, Daniel, we can sing it again."

At that moment, Hannah stormed into the auditorium.

"How dare you talk to me like that! She has less of a voice than me, and you chose to sing with her, not me! You are so pathetic, all of you."

Sarah put her head down and walked a few steps back.

Daniel walked to the front of the stage and spoke kindly to her. "Music and singing are more than the voice and acting. Worship service is for God's glory and is an act of love, humility, passion, commitment, team work and much more. Pray about it, and when you understand this, you can come back and talk to me and to us about worship."

Hannah wanted to say something else, but Jim took her aside and said gently, "Hannah, let's go and have a talk."

Meanwhile, Sarah started walking off the stage as she felt so embarrassed. Daniel looked around.

"Sarah, please come back. You have a beautiful voice and you promised you would sing with us today. Please do not run away again." He was almost begging her but waiting to see her reaction.

Sarah stopped. It was true, she had promised. She slowly turned and came back onto the stage. Daniel took her hand and could sense that she was a bit scared. He gave her the microphone and whispered, "You are the person the Lord chose to sing with us. Sarah, I would rather be here than anywhere else in the world."

She looked at him shyly with big eyes and managed, "Thank you, Daniel."

It took her some time to relax, but the music was flowing and she was carried away. It was such a blessed time.

As she was getting ready to leave, she felt it had been a good day after all. She was quite proud of herself for overcoming her anxieties.

Thomas came to speak to her.

"Hey, Sarah, are you leaving? Would you like to join us for lunch?"

She was not sure and looked at Maria. She felt she was not quite ready to join them. It might be best to take one step at a time.

Everyone was insisting she came, but she politely refused. "No, thank you. I have other plans for today. Maybe next time."

She had used that phrase so often…

As they were all leaving and chatting, Maria said, "Maybe we can catch up tomorrow? What do you think?"

"Yes, of course!"

As she got into the car, she caught Daniel's eyes. He was leaving with his friends. He smiled and waved to her. And that was just the beginning of something beautiful and unexpected.

Chapter 13

The Eagles

It was a beautiful day, and Daniel got up really early. His sister was coming to church with her two beautiful angels. It was Sunday, and Sarah was singing, or at least he hoped she would as she had promised and he loved singing with her. As he got ready, he looked twice in the mirror.

He chose a nice pair of dark blue jeans with a lovely black leather belt and a blue shirt with an open collar. He was pleased with the result, but when they got into the car, Katie asked, "Where is your guitar, Daniel?"

He laughed sheepishly. He would never forget his guitar – except today. He was more worried about how he looked than having his guitar. He rushed back for it and was so nervous that he asked his sister three times how he looked.

"You are very handsome, today! Isn't he, girls?"

"Yes, Uncle Daniel, you are so handsome. We love you."

At Grace Church, Daniel was not overly concerned about Katie as she was finding her way and making friends. He was the first of the Eagles there and started to check the equipment with the sound team, moving around impatiently.

"He is here – I can't believe it!" said Mark.

"It must be important," added Ruth.

Sarah showed up the same time as the others, 15 minutes before the service was due to start.

Daniel kept making sure everyone knew their turns.

Mark was singing the first two songs, followed by Thomas and Ruth, and then he was singing Surrender with Sarah.

He looked around the room and did not see her. He panicked.

"Where is Sarah?"

A voice near him said, "I am here!"

"Oh, good. I was afraid you would not show up today!"

He showed her the list of songs and explained to her when their turn would be.

"Are you sure you will be able to sing today?"

"Yes, Daniel!"

He gestured towards the people who were starting to come into the auditorium.

"Today is a special day, and there will be lots of people."

"It will be fine, Daniel. You know, I do pray as well." She smiled.

The band gathered to pray together, and Thomas gently pulled Sarah into the circle. The program started with all the announcements, followed by Bible verses, prayers and then worship.

Katie was sitting in the front row, with Margaret next to her. She had left the girls at the children's group, and Jane enjoyed looking after them. There was a ministry group of lovely, dedicated people who took turns to look after the children.

The first few songs went smoothly, and it was a lovely, encouraging time. The auditorium was full of people, including many visitors who had come for the special preaching service.

When it was their turn, Daniel moved to the front. Where was Sarah? She was next to him, and he breathed a sigh of relief. He started the song and she followed him, their voices harmonising beautifully.

Katie in the front row was proud of her brother.

Jim whispered something into Margaret's ear, and they looked very serious.

When Daniel was singing and playing, he was in another world. He had a powerful voice and was an anointed leader. He was flying like an eagle. When the song was over, he was so filled with joy that he briefly closed his eyes.

Once off the stage, all the Eagles were talking about the wonderful worship service. Thomas and Ruth had done a very good job, as they had never sung alone before, and Daniel and Sarah had been quite remarkable.

Daniel saw Sarah sitting in a corner on a chair. She was a bit lost in her thoughts. He walked toward her and said sincerely, "Thank you for today, Sarah! You were fantastic." He leaned over and kissed her on the cheek.

"We saw you," laughed Mark.

"Yes, of course you did!" Daniel seemed not to be bothered.

She smiled at him and he noticed her beautiful green eyes were very tired.

"Are you OK?"

"I think I might need a glass of water. I suddenly feel very tired."

He fetched her a glass of water, and even when the preaching started, he stayed with her backstage till she felt better. They sat in silence next to each other on a couple of chairs and listened to the service.

"Interesting way to listen to the preaching."

"That's no other place I would rather be, Sarah. Just here with you."

She looked at him, surprised, and blushed. He noticed and smiled. Maybe he enjoyed her company more than he thought. And it did not bother him to wait with her; he wanted to be with her. He hadn't felt like that in a long time.

The preaching that day was by Terry Brink. Terry was a good friend of Jim's and had been a member of the church for many years.

He was a widower in his late 60s and was dedicated to serving the Lord. He organized the Children's Ministry and Orphans' Support Group which worked with a variety of charities.

Afterwards, Jim walked to the back and caught up with the Eagles, who were in the little coffee room.

"My children!" said Jim.

"Hello, Jim!"

"What a blessed worship time!"

All looked very pleased and agreed.

"Daniel, and of course all of you, I keep asking for a Saturday worship hour. Are you going to give me an answer?"

Mark looked at Daniel.

"Come on, Daniel. We all said yes and we are all waiting for you!"

Daniel smiled and looked a bit serious. "Am I the last to say yes?"

Jim did not give up. "My son, one hour of worship. You know many in the church have requested it. Did you pray about it...? Did you ask the Lord?"

The others started laughing.

When it was about the Lord, it would take Daniel quite a while to get back with an answer, even if the Lord had given him the answer. He always wanted to make sure he'd heard correctly from the Lord. And he seemed sometimes not to be in a hurry, which seemed to contradict his joyful, impetuous character.

His mind was distracted as Sarah entered the little coffee room.

"Oh, yes, of course. I prayed. OK, Jim, I surrender! You can announce it – we'll start next Saturday. But before..."

"Oh, no! He's doing it again," said Ruth.

"We will try it for a month and see how it goes. Then we will decide whether to carry on with the program, OK?"

Jim was pleased, then seeing Sarah getting a drink, he continued.

"Are you going to ask Sarah to join your team for regular Sunday worship? Not only for practice?"

He was not sure he wanted to ask her. She seemed pretty good at saying no, and he did not think she was ready for it, but Jim seemed to push it.

"Would you like to join the Eagles, Sarah?"

Looking at her, he was sure she would say no. It had been hard enough to convince her to sing one song with him. He did not want to end up begging her for each song or chasing after her. He turned his face away, then heard her say, "I would love to!"

"It's settled, then," said Jim. "She is in. Daniel?"

All said yes and waited for Daniel, who turned around looking very serious.

"He is serious again," they teased.

"Daniel, what do you think?"

Sarah was 2 meters from him and she'd said yes!

He was not sure it was a good idea and he did not want to babysit her. Looking at her seriously, he said, "Sarah, this is a worship team. We are committed in prayer, working together for God's glory. We select songs to learn, we practice, we sing, we worship. We are committed. The kind of worship we bring is not just any kind. We are like a family. Can you keep up with us as it is not easy – it is challenging?"

"Daniel is right, it is a serious commitment."

Sarah looked at each one of them, then put her head down, feeling shy, but she did not want to give up.

During the past weeks, a desire to be part of the team had birthed in her heart. She kept praying about it and kept waiting to hear from the Lord.

"It would be an honour for me to serve the Lord and be part of the Eagles as I have been praying about it. However, Daniel, you are right. Could I really keep up with you?" She raised her head and looked straight into Daniel's eyes.

There was silence for a moment and tension between the two of them. Daniel waited for her to continue.

"Could I please try, Daniel? Team?"

"Welcome to the Eagles, Sarah!" said all the others, and everyone was waiting for Daniel again.

How could he say no? Easily! This was not about music... it was more. It was worship!

In his heart, he was not convinced she would be able to keep up with them, but he was willing to give her a chance.

"All right Sarah, you can try!"

He believed she would be a challenge for him, and he did not want to be slowed down by her and have to keep telling her to get back on stage or to sing. He wanted someone who could stand on their own feet. That remained to be seen.

However, something in her behaviour was so sweet, and each time she got shy, she made him smile. She started to be on his mind quite a lot, and he looked forward to singing with her at the weekends. Or was he just looking forward to seeing her? But he was not in the mood for meditating on the emotional side of things. At least, not for now.

Chapter 14

Jack, my best friend

As I'd promised Jack, I met him today. I was very surprised that he did not meet me at his house. He did say over the phone it was something very important.

Jack Curry had been my best friend since I was a kid. I still remember the time when my parents sold our family house and I felt so sad having to move into a new neighbourhood.

I felt strange and lonely the first few weeks, but Jack looked after me and introduced me to his friends. Throughout the years, we have remained friends.

Yes, he did get married, and I was his best man at the wedding.

Yes, we used to meet quite often, and sometimes we went jogging.

And then today, I met him again.

"Hey, Jack, nice to see you!"

"Daniel, you still have your messy hair. But it looks good on you. I could not imagine you otherwise."

Jack Curry was tall, dark-haired and wearing a smart shirt. He always looked so tidy, as if he'd come from the office. He loved his suits and shirts.

We were not at Rosie's but at Quick and Go. It was quite a good restaurant that could serve you a very good lunch in 10 minutes.

"Why here?" I asked.

"At the moment, things are a bit shaky in my house. Give me a few weeks and see what happens. Things are not good with Maria."

I looked at him, puzzled.

"We've tried counselling, and a couple of years ago she moved out."

It made me feel sad: Katie and Jack, both going through similar things, and it was not something that I wished to go through.

I shook my head unhappily.

"But, Daniel, look at me. I am OK, believe me!"

"I wish I could believe you."

"We managed some sort of agreement in the past, but now she wants the divorce and there you go."

He opened a folder and put some papers neatly on the table.

"She's decided to move to Australia!"

My heart felt like breaking all over again. I was already going through a lot of things with Katie. I did not need Jack as well. But he was doing a pretty good job looking after the boys and himself.

"Let's sign the divorce papers together. I will use you as a witness, OK?"

"Why did you not say anything, Jack? I could have helped. I thought you two were on the mend."

Jack smiled sadly. "My marriage was gone years ago, but I did not admit it and let go. It's time to let go now. You know Maria always got her own way, and things just got worse."

"And the boys?"

"The boys convinced me to let go. Otherwise, I possibly would not have done it. They'll be 15 soon. The good part is that they're already living with me, so we do not have to move. Mark found a job, and Peter is at his college and studying. So both my sons are on their feet with some sort of job."

"Where is Maria now?"

"She is leaving this week for Australia and wants money – there you go!" Jack seemed to accept the situation and was quite calm.

A lady brought sandwiches to their table.

"Can I bring you anything else, boys?"

"No, thank you. That is fine."

Turning back to his friend, he said, "Peter suggested not telling you as you might overreact!"

I had to laugh. "Yes, I always overact, don't I? Your sons know me – I am pretty passionate and forward sometimes, aren't I"

"Changing the subject, how are things with your sister? Are you still helping her? What about you?"

"Katie is going through an awful divorce. She did not want me to share this with anyone for a while. Now, finally, as you said, she is letting go, but it's not as smooth as yours. James is not very nice and asks for money; he is still in the house and you cannot negotiate with him. And it's Uncle Daniel to the rescue!"

"You must have lots on your plate."

"Well, I do not have my own family and I liked my silence and my music. Now it's extra noisy since Katie moved in with me, and her little ones, five and seven years old, are like little angels. Adorable nieces."

We carried on chatting about lots of other things.

"Are you watching the race this week? You can come to mine as usual!"

"Why not? When is it?"

"Thursday."

The phone rang and a voice asked, "Mr. Anderson? We are calling you from the hospital..."   I hardly heard the voice at the other end and I hung up in less than a minute.

"Are you all right?"

"Katie was... in an accident. She is in hospital. I have to go, Jack. You sort out the bill."

"Can I do anything?"

"At this point, nothing, but I will give you a shout if I need you. I need to go..."

My phone rang again or was I imagining it?

The hospital did not say much, and that concerned me. The girls, where were the little angels? Oh, my! I put my hand on my chest as a pain stabbed at my heart. Were they OK? I wondered whether they had been with her in the car, but the hospital mentioned only her. I took a deep breath and said a short prayer. The phone rang again, and I finally answered.

"Daniel, we have your nieces with us!" said Margaret.

"Thank you, Jesus!" I whispered.

"Sarah and I took them for a little lunch, and we could not get hold of Katie. Can we drop them at the house? Are you home?"

"Thank you, Lord, thank you." I kept saying it, then realized I was on the phone.

"Margaret, I am not home. Katie was in a car crash and I am on my way to the hospital. You have a key. Please go in and give me a hand with the girls. You know – dinner, bath... I will get back as soon as I can."

"Oh, my goodness! We will look after them. Please drive safely. Sarah is with me. We will look after them; do not worry."

"Thank you."

There were so many things going on and too much for me to process. Music, yes, music always helped me to calm down and sit peacefully at Jesus' feet. That is what I needed, but I was not even near my home.

At the front desk of the hospital, I was told where to go and I found the ward. The staff were very nice, but I wanted to see Katie. They showed me in. It was so quiet. So many little beeps and so many needles. I took a chair and sat near her, quietly.

"My Father in heaven, my Lord, Please help my sister. In the name of Jesus, I ask for healing. I believe and declare that by Your stripes we have been healed. My sister Katie is healed..."

I stayed silent for a long time. It started to get dark and still I sat there, praying from time to time, but mostly just holding her hand. A nurse came and checked on her, then a doctor entered and spoke to me in a low voice.

"Mr. Anderson, would you like to come with me so we can talk?"

I followed him and we had a talk, or he talked and I listened.

"Your sister is out of danger. I understand you are her brother. You do not need to worry; she is just on sedatives and has some bruises. We will keep her in hospital for a few days to make sure that she is out of danger."

"Thank you."

"She should be awake tomorrow if you plan to visit her. Should anyone else be informed? Does she have a family?"

"She lives with me; she is separated. She has two little daughters. I will be looking after my nieces." I cannot remember much more of the conversation. As I left the hospital, I looked at my watch. It was already late. I felt tired and hungry. What a day! I could not think and did not want to think. I could hardly wait to get home. Yes, my peaceful home.

Chapter 15

At home with you

Finally, I was at home and parked the car on the driveway. It took me some time to get out of the car. I could not think, my body felt tired, I just wanted quietness, and for sure, home was not quiet now. I noticed Margaret's car; of course, she was there.

As soon as I walked in, the two little angels ran toward me. "Uncle Daniel, Uncle Daniel, you are home! Where is Mummy?"

Margaret was in the kitchen cooking, and it was smelling good.

I picked up my nieces and gave them a cuddle, then carried them to the couch in the lounge.

"What have you been up to today, angels?"

"We had so much fun! We loved it. Where is Mummy?"

"Your mummy is having a little rest. She was not feeling well and she..."

Margaret showed up and helped. "She is resting in the hospital for a few days and sends her love to you. She will be home soon, won't she, Daniel?"

I sat back on the couch and whispered, "Thank you!"

The girls ran to the dining table.

"Let's colour something for Mummy," said May.

"Yes, yes, a butterfly!"

"No, she likes flowers..."

Margaret came to sit next to me. I sank into the couch and remembered that I still had my shoes on. I pulled them off and lay back for a minute with closed eyes.

"Did you have a hard day, Daniel?"

"You could say that. I don't want to talk about it, not yet."

Then I turned to her and smiled.

"But you know, I am absolutely starving!"

"Some things never change about you!" she said, laughing.

I could not deal with the noise, even if my nieces were sweet, so I went upstairs.

"Dinner in 20 minutes!" Margaret called.

I managed to have a shower and calmed down, at least. My brain was not processing anything and my heart was aching. I put on a pair of jeans and a white t-shirt and went straight to the music room in search of my guitar.

I sat on one of the chairs and started playing a slow song of worship. Once I'd finished, I sat quietly at Jesus' feet, listening to the Spirit and receiving comfort and strength.

After some time, I walked through the room and stopped in front of the window. It was getting dark and the street lights were on. It was very quiet and peaceful out there and it was peaceful in my heart. I felt refreshed. A lot of things had happened today.

There was a knock at the door, and as I said yes, the door opened slowly.

"Margaret is calling us for dinner!" said a shy voice.

It was Sarah, in my room. Of course, Margaret had mentioned that she was helping her look after the girls this afternoon. I'd forgotten about that.

"Sarah, come in, please! This is my music room."

I had been hoping to invite her for dinner one day, but well, this was something unexpected and out of my hands. My life did not always go as planned, which made things more interesting and kept me on my toes.

"Thank you for helping Margaret look after my nieces."

"Oh, I enjoyed spending time with them. They are adorable."

She looked around the room at the instruments, mostly guitars, and the sheets of music. I told her the story of each guitar, especially my favourite, a light brown one that had carried me through many situations.

Sarah noticed a piano keyboard and sat down in front of it. She touched it lightly, wanting to play, but changed her mind and withdrew her hands. *Make music to my heart, Oh, Lord!* She suddenly stood up. "This is a very bad idea for me."

I took a chair next to her and asked, "How long since you played?"

"More than 10 years. I used to have one like this… then one day it was gone. Living with my parents was not always easy. It was a long time ago. Let's go for dinner."

"I did not know you could play. I want to hear you play, Sarah."

"As I said, it has been a long time. Maybe another time, Daniel."

"You need to forgive and let go of the past. So you can move on! Beauty for ashes, Sarah."

Something got her attention and she turned her big beautiful green eyes toward me. "Will you please play with me?"

I smiled. "Of course." I sat next to her and we played.

She closed her eyes and touched the keys gently. She played quite a sad love song and I followed her.

When she'd finished, I saw a tear running down her cheek and was not sure how should I react. I would have liked to give her a hug, but I did not move.

"It was beautiful, Sarah."

Then I gently took over and played a happy song.

"Let me show you music, girl!"

To my surprise, she joined me and we both had fun. She was smiling again.

"You know, Daniel, you are really... really..."

"Yes?"

"You are an amazing man! And maybe crazy, sometimes. You do push me to the limits."

She made me laugh as everything she said was true.

A voice called from the door, "You two musicians, dinner, please. The girls are already eating."

As we walked out the room, Sarah suddenly stopped, turned around and said, "Thank you for the music you brought back into my life."

We went downstairs and joined the girls, and we all had fun. We heard the doorbell, and I went and opened the door. There was Jane.

"Hello, oh... you are having your dinner. I just came to see if Sarah needed a lift home."

"Yes, please, that would be good as I am working tomorrow."

She sat down and joined us for a cup of tea while we finished our dinner.

"So, who is for bath time this evening?"

The girls jumped and said, "Uncle Daniel, Uncle Daniel!"

I smiled but was not sure I was in the mood for bath time.

"Do you want me to give you a hand?" said Jane.

"Two hands, please. I have to work tomorrow and I have quite a lot to do."

Margaret talked with Jane as they cleared the table. The girls went upstairs and Sarah sat on the couch, looking at some of my CDs. My phone rang and it was Jack, asking about Katie, which was nice of him. I hung up and got back to Sarah.

"So, when are we going to look for a house for you?"

"It's up to you. I am mostly free at lunchtime this week."

"Hmm, I will call you. Let me see how I am for lunches. I am usually on site in the afternoon with the boys. But you never know with me, where I am I and what's come up."

"Yes, I noticed that, Daniel."

Margaret came and sat down in an armchair.

"Daniel, I've spoken to Jane. Shall we organize to collect your nieces from school for a few days?"

"That would be great, as I am working and I'll need to go to the hospital. It is getting a bit complicated. Thank you."

"Leave it with me... Between Jane and I and the Help Team, we'll organize dinner and stay here till you get back from work."

"You are an angel!" and I stood up and gave her a kiss.

"So, how is Katie?"

"Katie is fine and out of danger. She was under sedation and the doctors will let me know more tomorrow."

"That is good. You are doing a very good job, Daniel. You have a good heart, taking her and your nieces into your house and looking after them."

"What else can I do? I'm just being me."

It had been such a tiring day, but in the end pretty good, and I had a lovely time with Margaret, Jane, my nieces and, of course, Sarah.

Sarah was quite a mystery to me. I enjoyed her company, but she was so different from all the other ladies I'd met.

She certainly had a gift for music, and that was something that we had in common. We both loved music and were passionate about singing. But it was something more with Sarah; yes it was more about her.

My nieces were already bathed and in bed. I lay on the couch, stretched out and listened to the music playing softly until I fell asleep.

Chapter 16

Dinner

The week passed quickly, and I was busy at work and at home. Katie was able to come home on Wednesday, and the girls were happy to have her back with us, but we still had Margaret and Jane passing by and helping us, which was very kind of them. They were really good.

On Saturday, I managed to get to our practice, but I was late, and we also had our Saturday worship for an hour afterwards. I was still not sure how it would work out but was willing to try it. All of us were there, including Sarah, and she even sang a few songs with me.

The Eagles decided to go out for lunch, and we asked Sarah to join us. She refused, which did not surprise me.

I was ready to leave with my guitar when I heard a voice behind me.

"Daniel, can I talk with you please?"

Surprised, I turned around. "Yes, of course."

She kept looking down, so I decided to start.

"Yes, Sarah?"

I was in a bit of a hurry as I had also planned to meet Jack later and I'd promised Katie I would cook dinner as well.

"Could I have some of your songs, please, so I can practise them once I get a keyboard?"

"Really? You want to practise some songs at home?"

Getting her confidence, she said, "Yes, I would like that."

"Look, I am in a rush. I have to go. But I will give them to you during the week."

"Ah, there were other things I wanted to talk to you about."

"Come by for lunch tomorrow at my office, like 12 o'clock. Would that be all right for you? We can talk then. What do you say?"

"All right, Daniel. I will see you tomorrow."

We all had fun at Rosie's restaurant, but I had to excuse myself from the group.

"I must leave now. I have shopping to do – I am cooking tonight!"

"How do you do it all?!"

"Thomas, I really do not know, but I take one day at a time. And grace, grace!"

"How is your sister feeling?" asked Ruth.

"She is home and much better, thank you. She will return to work next week."

Driving home, I thought of Sarah and her lack of a piano. I remembered my little old shop where I bought all kinds of things, and then I asked my Lord, "What shall I do, my Lord? Shall I buy her a keyboard?" And I heard the soft voice of the Holy Spirit in my heart saying *Yes*.

As I left the shop, I was so happy. What would Sarah say and how would she react? "Shyly!" He smiled.

I managed to be home by 4.00 and had actually forgotten about Jack.

"I am home with the shopping!"

A voice came from the lounge. "I am here!" Jack laughed. "Tell me you didn't forget I was coming at 3.00!"

"Yes, I did, Jack. Sorry, I had other things on my mind."

Katie was in the dining room.

"Do not worry. I was looking after Jack, and it's always nice to see him."

May and Ella were happy to see Uncle Daniel and jumped on me.

"Can we help you cook the dinner, please, Uncle Daniel?"

Katie jumped in protectively.

"No, that's really not a good idea."

"Of course you can, my little helpers. Come here. Let me give you a big hug."

"Can we?"

"Of course you can – OK, Mummy?"

Katie did not have a choice but to agree, so the little angels were happy.

Turning toward Jack, Katie said, "You see what I have to put up with? Daniel always says yes to them. I keep telling him to have his own family. I believe he would be a lovely daddy. Don't you think so, Jack?"

"That is quite a no for me. Not now. Maybe one day... maybe."

Jack spoke up. "You've been saying that for the last few years now."

Whenever Katie or Jack or anyone else asked about girls or dating, I would just turn the conversation around. It was not something I wanted to speak about or even cared about.

The evening went well. I had not heard my sister laughing for a long time. Jack left at 7.00 and Katie had put the girls to bed. I felt tired and went into my music room.

Then Katie knocked at the door.

"Daniel, I spoke to Jack. He advised me on a few things regarding my divorce. I hope it is OK if he helps me sort out some issues with my solicitor. I thought you had enough on your plate with us living here with you and you helping me so much."

"Katie, Jack is a very nice man, and I am not saying that because he is my friend. Yes, it is a good idea."

Alone again, I worshipped in silence. I knew so many "I love you Lord" songs. I ended up talking to the Lord. To me, prayer was not just praising the Lord, asking, declaring, breaking chains, receiving, but also talking to Him as a friend.

I remembered that the first time I prayed, I did not know what to do or say. Jim said, "Talk to the Lord. He is your Father, your Saviour, your Lord, your best friend. He loves to hear your voice and your heart; he loves to be with you, help you, guide you and bless you with joy, love, peace, wisdom, patience, grace. And his blessings are not only spiritual, for your soul, but they overflow into your life. Day by day, spend time with your Father and He will help you. Ask boldly – your Father loves you!"

My phone pinged and it was a message from Sarah.

"Hello, Daniel. I am really sorry but I already have other commitments tomorrow for lunch and I did not realize that. I spoke to Jane, and she thought it might be a good idea for you to come for dinner tomorrow evening at 600. Please let me know if that would be OK for you. If you have other plans, we can sort out another day."

I was a bit surprised but decided to accept the dinner offer.

* * *

"Good evening handsome one!" Jane gave him a big hug.

Daniel gave her a big bouquet of flowers.

"You have not lost your touch, young man. Come in, come in."

"Hello Sarah," he said. As he entered, he remembered something and rushed out back to the car.

"I will be right back."

He walked back in with the beautiful new keyboard.

"This is for you, Sarah." He smiled and gave it to her.

She was not sure how to react.

" I … I thank you. You should not have... thank you."

Over the past few months, Daniel had come to know her better and got used to her shy moods. He thought they were sweet.

"That is nice, Sarah! Daniel, are you trying to impress my little Sarah?"

Daniel stayed for dinner, but the conversation was mostly between him and Jane as Sarah was very quiet.

Finally, Jane said to her, "You need to speak up, girl, otherwise we will have Daniel every day of the week and I am sure he is very busy and has other plans. Or do you feel it is Christmas with Daniel giving you such a nice gift? It must have cost a few pounds, boy!"

"Anything for Sarah. She deserves much better, but this is what I could find at the moment."

Sarah blushed and changed the subject.

"Yes, Daniel, I want to buy a new house, as you know, and I need help with it. You told me to let you know when I wanted things to move. Now I am ready."

He knew he had quite a busy week ahead and was not sure where he could fit Sarah into his schedule.

"Let me think about it. Give me a week and I will talk to some of my friends. I'll get back to you, and next week we can maybe go and view some properties. What do you think?"

"Yes, that would be good, thank you. Are you coming with me?"

He looked at her, surprised, not sure he understood the question. He had not planned to go with her. He had to slow down with his work as things were getting too much for him and he needed a few days off to rest.

"Do you want me to come?"

"I would like you to come with me. I would like to know your opinion."

She took a piece of paper and wrote some details regarding the house she was looking for, such as the price. He got lost for a moment in his thoughts as he helped Jane to clear the table. Suddenly he decided to leave. He apologised and was gone in 10 minutes.

He decided to go for a drive. He felt the Holy Spirit wanted him to listen, and he loved to sit at Jesus' feet and learn all kinds of things. The Lord always taught him and gave him insight and revelation, and he loved studying his Bible and meditating on God's word.

He drove for more than an hour and returned home quite late, but Katie was used to his comings and goings and never knowing where he was.

Chapter 17

A new home

On Saturday, Sarah did not go to practice and she had not contacted Daniel. He wondered whether she was upset that he had not called her; he had been too busy, but he had spoken to some of his friends regarding houses. The thought that she might be "running away" again also crossed his mind.

Suddenly, one of the doors opened and Jim came in. He walked straight to the stage and made a sign to Daniel, who jumped down in a second.

"Daniel, Sarah just called to say she was not feeling well. She has a bad cold and is not sure whether she can make it tomorrow. She asked me to let you all know that she is sorry not to be here. She is actually in bed."

"Thank you, Jim."

Daniel gave his band the news and they all agreed to pray for her.

On the way home, he thought about calling her but changed his mind Maybe she was resting and did not want to talk to anyone, or maybe she just did not want to talk to him.

Daniel went home and had a quiet afternoon. He watched a film, which was quite unusual for him. Katie was out with the girls.

Actually, Jack had asked her to go to his house for dinner and offered to help her with the girls. His kids were much older and were out a lot.

The phone rang and Margaret was at the other end.

"Daniel, oh, good. I caught you! I was wondering if you could give us a hand. Patrick and Martha are busy, and I have to rush to the hospital to visit a lady. Totally unexpected. I was wondering if you could pop round to see Sarah Grant."

He was listening to see what Margaret was up to.

"Jane is out of town for a couple of days visiting her sister. I promised Sarah I'd pop round with some shopping for her and some food."

He was not sure whether he wanted to pop round and see Sarah. That was quite unexpected. Hmm.

However, he said, "Yes, I will go and do a little shopping and drop it at her house and check on her."

Margaret was happy and grateful. Daniel, on the other hand, had to get out and even go shopping.

Stretching and taking his time, he finally moved and went to a little Express Shop and then to Rosie's for a takeaway that he'd ordered before he left home. One hour later he was there, knocking at Sarah's door, but nobody answered. He kept knocking, and after 10 minutes he even called her cell phone. Nobody answered, so he decided to go in.

On a couch was Sarah, asleep with the TV on.

She had a blanket over her and a tissue box next to her.

There were lots of dishes in Jane's kitchen, so Sarah probably did not feel well enough to do anything. Daniel put the food in the kitchen and started to organize the dinner. Then he washed the dishes, which made a lot of noise and woke Sarah.

"Oh, Daniel! You're here!"

Smiling, he approached the couch and sat next to her.

It was obviously not a good move because she felt uncomfortable with him too close to her. She was breathing with difficulty through her stuffy nose, and her eyes looked tired.

He put his hand on her forehead.

"Good, you do not have a temperature. But you do have a red nose, Rudolf!"

"Thank you, Doctor Daniel."

He got up and walked toward the dining table.

"I brought some dinner from Rosie's. Would you like to join me at the dinner table or would you prefer your couch?"

"I will sit at the table, thank you. But what are you doing here? I thought Margaret was supposed to come."

Daniel pretended to be upset and waited to see her reaction.

"Do you want me to leave?"

"No, no. I'm just surprised that you're here. Please stay. It's nice to see you."

"Surprise! Ta, ta! It's me!" He laughed with open arms and did a bow, which made Sarah laugh.

Daniel arranged all the plates and served the food. He had chosen a hot soup as a starter, then a pasta dish with chicken and sauce. He organized everything attractively, and Sarah felt spoiled. He was chatty and told her lots of things about his work and also about the worship songs they'd played that morning.

"We missed you today!" he added.

"You did? That is good. I've been in bed all day."

He looked at her.

"I missed singing with you!"

She looked surprised and did not say a word.

She gradually relaxed and joined in the conversation. When she started sneezing, Daniel jumped up and brought the box of tissues. She smiled as she watched him. He was doing a good job of looking after her, and she enjoyed being spoiled.

"Are you going to look for a new house, Sarah?"

He took out his phone, drew his chair nearer to her and showed her some pictures of houses he had in mind for her.

Sarah immediately liked one of the houses. It was white with four bedrooms and a large garden.

"The price is too high, Sarah. I can talk to Mark Baker. He is one of my friends, and the company often uses his agency for business. Maybe he can bring the price down a bit."

Sarah was enthusiastic. "Could I view it on Monday?"

Considering she was not feeling well, Daniel was not sure that was a good idea.

"I could take you there, if you promise you'll feel better and up to it."

"Please arrange a viewing for Monday. I will be better, I promise."

Then looking down, she gently touched his hand. "Could you please come with me, Daniel?"

He smiled and took her hand into his. "Of course! But now let's take you back to your couch. Would you like some hot tea? Anything else?"

"No, thank you. It was very nice..."

From the kitchen, Daniel said, "Hope you are staying home tomorrow, but I will miss singing with you, and the Eagles will miss you too."

"Yes, I am, of course."

He looked at his watch.

"I will have to leave now. It is getting late for me and I have other things planned."

He gently covered her with a blanket. If you need anything, please call me. Otherwise, I will see you Monday if all goes well."

Sunday was totally different and Mark was the first to notice.

"Are you blue, Daniel, because Sarah is not here?"

Daniel tried to find an excuse, but the truth was that he was a little blue. Yes, he kind of missed her.

"I have a few things on my mind, so I won't join you today for lunch!"

On the way home from church, he thought about calling her but changed his mind again. Home alone, he drew near to the Lord and spent time in prayer. When it was about bold prayer, Daniel was pretty good and was not afraid to ask from the Father. He was courageous and always brought all his worries to the Lord. His was an open heart, filled with love and truth and a beautiful relationship with the Lord. He truly loved the Lord and always spent time listening to the promptings of the Holy Spirit. Yes, the wisdom of the Lord and the paths of the Lord often passed all his understanding. But he was not here to understand all things; he was here to ask and receive from the Lord.

What was his heart telling him regarding Sarah? That was a good question. Was she just a friend or was she becoming a bit more to him? He would have to figure out that. But she was a beautiful woman, a kind, gentle soul who brought him peace through her singing. Yes, she was quite a challenge for Daniel.

He was much more the flying spirit, passionate and on the go all the time. He differed totally in spiritual and physical strength. He was a leader and always brimming with new ideas.

But in music, they were like fire and water, complementing each other. They'd had the best worship services lately. God knew what He was doing, more than anyone else, for sure. Daniel had no clue what was he doing at that point.

And he was not in the mood to analyse how he felt towards Sarah. Not now, maybe another time. Sometimes the Lord had to give him a push, like an eagle mother throws her baby out of the nest. The babies learn to fly when they have not planned to. The mother catches them, takes them back into the nest and throws them again until they have learnt to fly. The mother knows when they are ready.

Yes, he had often needed to be thrown out of his nest by the Lord; otherwise, he would never have stretched in some areas. The Lord knew how to deal with him, and he loved it. It was such an adventure, even if it was hard. He always loved it when the Lord was testing him. He learnt from each situation and discovered where the Lord was taking him.

On Monday, Daniel was so busy that he forgot about Sarah until around noon.

"Becky, get me Mark Baker please."

"Now? He might be on his lunch break."

"Get him anyhow and anywhere he is, please. It is quite urgent."

About 30 minutes later, all was sorted out. He had arranged to view two of the houses, and one of them was the Little Cottage.

Later, when he picked Sarah up, she said, "I'm really looking forward to seeing the Little Cottage. Don't you think it is quite an interesting name for a four-bedroom property?"

Daniel was tired and was not feeling chatty. His phone rang again.

"Yes, Patrick. Of course. I can come, let's say after 6. Yes, see you then."

He hung up and was quiet.

"I'm sorry, Sarah, but I have been very busy and still have to go onto the site and see my boys after your house viewing."

The moment Sarah saw the Little Cottage, she fell in love with it.

"It is just me today," said Daniel. "Mark gave me the keys and we can look around. See what you think. It is a beautiful property."

Daniel could see that it needed some work, but it was not too bad, and it would not take long.

"What do you think Sarah?"

"I love it. Can I make an offer?"

"Yes, if you are sure. We can still go and view the others."

"No, no, I want to make an offer."

"All right, Sarah, and who will fix the house for you? It needs some upgrading."

Without hesitation, she said, "You, Daniel!"

"Me? Me... hmm!"

"I am sorry, I should have asked you first. Would you like to help me? Of course, I will pay..."

They were getting into the car and he did not give her an answer.

Sarah was quiet and felt bad.

"I have to take you home, and I need to go back to work, all right?"

As she got out of the car, he came around and walked her to the main door.

"Sarah, yes, I would love to fix your house. I'll organize things with my team and will get back to you about the house price. Please be patient – I have quite a lot to sort out."

"Thank you, Daniel." As he was ready to leave, she smiled and did something unexpected. She kissed him on the cheek. That was crossing a boundary – for both Sarah and Daniel!

Daniel smiled in surprise.

"I'll send the offer for the house tomorrow."

Driving away, Daniel kept thinking of Sarah. But he shook off the thoughts that started to flood his mind and spoke to the Lord.

"I hope you don't get me into a relationship, Lord, and yes... love!" He laughed.

Daniel had not been planning anything like this. However, Sarah had managed to cross some of his heart's boundaries, and maybe, in a way, he was wrestling with God. He was hiding behind his work without taking a moment to discern the truth and what the Lord was doing in his life and in his heart.

Yes, the boundaries of his heart.

Chapter 18

Friendship?

I woke up in the night and could not sleep, so I started to play my guitar. After half an hour, I decided to go into the lounge and play some worship music. Sitting at Jesus' feet always brought me peace, clarity and understanding. I heard a noise and it was Katie coming to check on me.

"Are you all right, Daniel?"

"Yes, I am fine, thank you. I just came down as I could not sleep."

"It's not like you to get up in the middle of the night. Are you worrying about anything? Do you have too many projects at work?"

I did not want to get into a conversation so gave a short excuse and went back to my bedroom. Much better than having an hour-long debate with Katie. She was pretty good at that, and from there she would probably have gone into her own problems, which I had already heard over and over.

I had to admit that lately she had started to look forward to leaving the past behind, and my friend Jack was doing a good job of looking after her as well.

When the alarm clock rang early in the morning, I felt so tired I did not even move. But at the third ring, I jumped out of bed and rushed to work. I felt so tired throughout the day that I bought a takeaway and went to eat in the park. I had not done that for months. The wind blew through my hair, and the fresh air was a bit too cold, but that did not bother me. I stayed there for more than an hour, just looking at the trees, the birds and occasional passers-by. I started meditating and my thoughts went straight to Sarah.

We had met quite frequently lately in all kinds of situations, not only at church. I remembered the first song she sang and smiled. Things had moved on a bit; she was part of the Eagles now and was singing many songs, and yes, was singing with me. I remembered when I had given her the keyboard and how happy she had been. It probably felt like Christmas to her. I laughed thinking of it.

That evening, back in my bedroom, I threw myself on the bed and fell asleep straight away. I did not hear Katie knocking at the door. She must have come in and covered me up. I woke up the next day feeling much refreshed.

At work, Mark Baker called and told me that the owners of the Little Cottage had accepted Sarah's offer.

"Thank you, Mark. Sarah will be so happy to hear that. I shall let her know."

Sarah was at work when I phoned to give her the news.

"Oh, I can't believe it! I am so happy. Oh, my goodness. Let me know what the next steps are and what do I need to do, please."

"I will let you know. I am very happy for you, Sarah."

It got really quiet and she said, "I could not have done it without the Lord, for sure. But I also want to thank you."

"No problem, girl! Look, I have to go. I shall see you Saturday!"

"Yes, of course!"

The week seemed to fly by, and for some reason, I was not looking forward to the coming Saturday. I went, anyway.

The Lord had been prompting me to sit down and be truthful to my own heart, but I kept delaying it and keeping myself busy. I knew what the Lord wanted me to talk about with Him, but I did not want to have that chat. Maybe I would, but not now.

I had a very good life and was not in the mood to change. I had never even thought about any other kind of life. A new lifestyle was certainly not in my prayers.

Sarah came to both the practice and the worship hour on Saturday.

Jim and Margaret invited me to their house after the Sunday worship service, and I accepted the invitation. On the way there, I wondered what it was about as it seemed I was the only one invited, but you never knew with the Carters. Things were always on the move, with people coming and going like a house of blessings.

"Nice you managed to come, Daniel!"

I walked into the lounge where Margaret was serving the tea.

"Hello, Daniel. How are you?"

"Hello, Margaret, I am very well, thank you."

"I shall make some quick sandwiches and join you as soon as I've finished."

I sat down, a little curious.

"Well, Jim, is it just me today? This must be serious. What have I done? Am I in trouble?" I smiled.

Jim brought his Bible and started as usual with prayer, thanking God and asking the Lord for wisdom and peace and guidance.

Margaret joined us and we enjoyed a simple, quick lunch.

All was quiet and I asked straight out, "So what is this about, Jim and Margaret? I see you quite often, but it must be very important if it's just you and me!"

"Nothing to worry about, son!"

"We just wanted to see how you were doing."

"Brick Houses is doing well," I replied.

"That's good." Margaret looked pleased.

"There are lots of projects and they keep me busy. You know, Jim – you usually come once a week and we catch up in the canteen and have a good chat and a laugh."

"Yes, Daniel, we do have good times together. You know, you have been such a blessing to Margaret and me, and the church."

"Thank you, Jim."

"The Lord really blessed us with you in our lives."

Changing the subject, Margaret said, "We heard you were working hard and you are on site every afternoon with the boys, often till late in the evening."

"I am with my boys almost every day. Many of them are my friends, and how can I understand them better unless I am one of them and spend time with them?"

Jim finished his lunch and rubbed his hands.

"Daniel, you are working very hard and also serving a lot at church. How about your private life?"

I felt amused as Jim was asking about my non-existent private life. At this point, my life revolved around Katie, sometimes Nick, 100% work, serving at church and yes, worship and music.

"Oh, my private life. You know Katie is living with me and those lovely angels, my nieces. My house is noisy but I love them all. Her divorce is nearly through. They seem to have reached an agreement and they will be signing the papers this coming week."

"All is good, then, with her, Daniel?"

"Yes, I am looking for her to move into another property as they will sell the family house. I offered to cover part of the house payment as she won't be able to cover it by herself."

"That is very good of you, Daniel. Always there for others. What about you?"

"I am fine, Jim. Why so much worry about me?"

"Do you ever think about having a family of your own, Daniel?"

"No, Margaret, it is not the first thing on my prayer list at the moment. I am quite enjoying my life the way it is. Not sure I want a family or am even ready for a family"

"You will never be ready unless you are willing to try."

I smiled.

"I've known you both for so many years. You are so dear to my heart, my lovely spiritual parents. You always look after me. What do you have on your mind?"

Both of them spoke at the same time:

"We were wondering what you thought about Sarah?"

"Hmm, Sarah. Yes, she is a nice girl!" Then I realized that they were asking whether I might be interested in her as a bit more than a friend.

I laughed. "That's why you called me here? To make sure I am not growing old alone? Really!"

Margaret smiled.

"Seems we've been caught out!"

Jim took over the conversation:

"We've heard lots of good things about her, and everybody is talking about how well-matched you two are. Yes, I was wondering whether you were interested in dating her?"

I looked down, then noticed that Margaret had left the room.

"I really like her as a friend. As for a relationship, I am not sure I want to get on that road again. I have not been thinking of relationships or girls, Jim. I am quite busy, you know. And also a girl like her might not want to accept a guy like me. But, yes, maybe I do like her more than I should."

Jim smiled.

"Yes, it's kind of hard to keep up with you; maybe you need to slow down. She is a very nice lady who has had quite a challenging life, and she found the Lord. I believe she is quite your opposite, don't you agree?"

Taking a big, deep breath, I realised I was having the conversation that the Lord had kept trying to have with me for the past weeks and I'd kept avoiding. The Lord always finds a way to help you be truthful to your heart. The Lord wanted to deal with this and it had to be done; Jim was here to make sure I actually confronted the issue.

"Daniel, my son, you are now 42, and if I were you, I would think seriously about my life. If you choose to live alone for the rest of your life, that is your choice. But I've always believed and prayed that the Lord would send you a good life partner, a lovely lady. You are an amazing man, and I want you to have the best of the Lord in your life. Don't you?"

The rest of the afternoon we talked about a lot of other things, including the fact that Sarah had bought a property. They were very happy for her. I did have to promise Jim that I would think about having a relationship and a family, and Sarah as well. After a very good afternoon, I was on my way home.

"My Lord, you do not give up on me, do you? You want me to meditate on relationships and things like that. OK, I surrender. I will pray and think about it and let your Spirit lead me. Seems you still want me to have a relationship, although I've fought against it so hard. It might be time for me to lay it at your feet and let Your will be done."

In the weeks after my conversation with Jim and Margaret, I met them regularly as usual and Jim was still coming to my canteen and having a chat with me and my friends.

It was a beautiful March day. The streets were green with the new leaves on the trees. The birds were building their nests and I was busy in my office.

The phone rang and I heard the voice of Mr. Green, the manager of Green Houses. He owned a big, well-known company in the west of England. Our paths had crossed before, and Brick Houses had worked with him on various projects. We had a good relationship and he always called me when something new came up.

"Hey Daniel, how are you?"

"Hello, Peter. Yes, we are keeping busy. How are you?"

"I have been thinking of you as we plan to expand again. We are talking about taking on more projects on the west coast.

I was not surprised as they were always extending their business.

"Glad to hear. So what's new?"

"Well, that is where you might come in, as usual. I have a project of 100 houses that might take six months or so. I need someone to work with me. I can email you the project and all the information."

"Thank you, Peter. That sounds quite good. I'll let you know what I think and where I stand."

I had once joined him in building a huge hotel resort on a beautiful beach on the west coast. We worked pretty well together, and I had a very good time. But that was some years ago. I had to travel and was away for three months.

But now I was part of the Eagles and was helping in the church and my life seemed to be going in another direction. Accepting a project like this would mean readjusting my life for six months.

Just then, Nick Palmer knocked at the door.

"Hey Daniel, can I come in? We need to talk about supplying materials and things, you know."

"Nick, give me 15 minutes please, then we can talk. I have to look through a project that I've just received."

Nick had learned to be adaptable as things were always on the go and you never knew what the next job might be.

"The Lord opens unexpected doors and provides new opportunities and challenges. Let's see what this is about," I whispered.

The proposal included all kinds of spreadsheets, from costs, to how many teams, the timing and materials required. It was very well done, and I was not so much concerned with the cost as with how many of my men I would need to take, as well as other reports of the area and the weather.

Yes, six months was quite a long time.

I picked up the phone and called my spiritual dad: Jim Carter.

"Hello, Jim! I was wondering whether you were coming to the canteen today?"

"Yes, son, I am coming. You know I am trying my best to come twice a week. I might get hired soon and work for you there..." He chuckled.

"Good, I need to talk to you. Something important has just come through."

"Of course; I shall see you at lunch."

I was early this time and was waiting for Jim.

When he arrived, he sat down and put his Bible on the table. Wherever Jim went, he had his Bible with him.

"You're very early!"

"Yes, I am. I'm looking forward to sharing something with you and getting your insight into the matter."

"Let's hear it. But first, let me get a drink and something to eat. You've already finished your lunch."

Jim went and said hello to the girls in the canteen and it took him 15 minutes to get back to the table.

"I love talking to the girls. And the food is delicious here."

"Yes, it is, and they are doing a very good job."

"Now, I am ready for you. Tell me, what news?"

"Jim, one of my friends invited me to be part of a big project. Not only me but a team of our boys. It is on the west coast. You remember Peter Green and his big company? We keep doing business with him."

"Oh, yes, I do remember and you travelled sometimes, working with him. What is on your mind, son?"

"Jim, it will be six months at least. And it's on the coast. You won't see me if I am leading part of the project or the entire project."

Jim stopped eating.

"Really? That is quite big! What are you building?"

"Houses, 100 at least!"

"That is a big project! So, you want prayers, and you need prayers, and?"

"I need your advice and to know what you think."

Jim looked at me and hesitated.

"Daniel, Daniel, my son. You always keep me on my toes. Now, I'm not sure you will like what I am about to tell you!"

"I am listening, Jim. I am listening."

"You know that I'll stand by you in whatever decision you take, whether I agree with you or not. Daniel, you need to decide what you want most in life. The Lord has brought you to a point where you might settle for the rest of your life or take other paths. This is like a test from the Lord and also a crossroads for you. You are all over the place, doing lots of things – your job, serving in the church, leading the worship team – and then there is your private life, if you have one, which I doubt."

"True, Jim. I do not have a private life."

"Many people embrace different paths and different situations and rush into all kinds of choices; they regret it afterwards and find themselves in various messes, or they regret they did not follow their heart and the path that was laid out in front of them."

He put his hand on his heart and took my hand in his other hand.

"My son, I would not like you to have a broken heart again or choose a wrong path. But the Lord has us all in His hands. Now, what would you choose?"

Tears welled up in my eyes as I knew Jim's heart and what he spoke was true.

I loved my job, but was that the path I would have chosen?

Church was my life; it was more like my home than my own house.

Private life, what private life? I was always on the go and now my private life had been invaded by Kate and my nieces. Going away would be quite a big change.

Jim waited for a few minutes then continued gently. "Daniel, wherever you go and whatever you do, there will always be challenges that will distract you from the Lord; tests and temptations. Whether you go or not, keep the Lord first. Follow Him and do not lose your passion. You have a gift that brings joy and hope to people. Your music touches hearts, and the Lord is using you in so many ways. My son, ask the Lord what He wants for you, which path to follow, and obey Him no matter how hard it is. You know, my son, you are greatly loved here in the church and also in your company. If you go, we will miss you, and we won't be able to replace you."

I stood and gave Jim a big hug and held him tight.

"Jim, after what you have said, I definitely want to stay. However, I'll have to pray about it and see what the Lord tells me."

Then Jim added, out of the blue, "There is also Sarah…"

"Who?"

"Sarah Grant. You have been singing with her quite a lot."

"Oh, no! Sarah, yes. She is quite a challenge for me."

"Now, Daniel, I will pray for you. Seems you have quite a lot on your plate. Once you have decided and have taken the first step, the Holy Spirit will take the next step with you, and like this, you will keep moving. The Lord will lead you. Be strong and courageous and do not give up. Keep going. Listen and follow your heart. The Lord is with you."

"Thank you, Jim!"

"I have to go, Daniel. I have to visit Maria at the hospital. Let me know once you have figured it out. I will be very interested to know which path you will choose to follow."

I did not share with my sister or Nick anything we had discussed. I felt a bit overwhelmed about it all. I prayed and meditated about it but still did not make a decision.

On Saturday, the Eagles had practice, then an hour of worship. It was quite busy, and almost the entire church was there.   Sarah looked very nice, not as if she was dressed for the office. She looked good in a red dress with short sleeves. It accentuated her beautiful emerald eyes. She was enthusiastic about the new songs I had chosen to sing with her.

"They are very good. I like Keep Going." She looked at me with her big eyes and asked, "Daniel, are you listening?"

She made me smile; actually, I was not listening. I was thinking of what Jim had said. *Me and her? Um…*

Since she had joined the Eagles, I had seen her quite a lot and enjoyed getting to know her better. She was a beautiful, gentle soul with a very kind heart. She was like a late-blooming flower, quite beautiful, especially when she smiled and her little dimples appeared. There was much to consider about Sarah.

"You are very quiet today, Daniel. Are you all right?"

"I am fine, Sarah; just some extra things on my mind."

Once the practice and the worship hour were over, I ran to catch Jim.

"Where are you going, Daniel? Are you not coming with us to Rosie's?"

"Not today, Mark. Sorry, I have other plans."

I ran as I saw Jim's car leaving and jumped in front of the car.

Jim slammed on the brakes.

"Daniel, do you want to give me a heart attack?"

"Jim, I have two or three days' leave. I was wondering whether I could have the key for the Red Cottage if no one is taking it next week."

"Yes, it is free. What do you have in mind? Some time alone with the Lord?"

"Exactly that. I plan to leave tomorrow after the worship service. And return Tuesday morning."

"No problem. I shall see you when you are back. May the Lord be with you and grant you peace and wisdom."

On Sunday morning, I was ready to leave straight after the service. Katie had found out only a couple of days before about my big project offer. I did not share anything else but did tell her that I would be away for a few days.

Katie had been getting a lot of support from Jack lately. They made a pretty good couple, and I thought they would soon be dating.

Friends at church asked me why I was going away, and I just said I needed a short break, but no one believed me.

As I was leaving the church, I almost bumped into Sarah.

"Are you leaving?"

"Yes, Sarah. I am not coming to Rosie's. I am going away for a few days."

She looked surprised as she was going to Rosie's this time.

"Really? Hope you have a good time."

I smiled. "Yes, I will. Will you pray for me, Sarah?"

"Yes, I will... I will!" She felt shy and I had to laugh.

As I got into my car, I felt my heart beating fast, and I saw Sarah driving just in front of me. I could not focus on the things I intended to think about; my mind was all over the place, and I did not even hear the music in the background, although it was so loud.

After 30 minutes on the highway, I turned left and drove for another hour. This was my favourite route, through green pastures and fields full of crops. The Red Cottage was a well-designed modern house with three bedrooms. It was used regularly by church members and sometimes by Margaret and Jim, who owned it.

I'd already done some shopping and was not planning to go out eating. I'd just bought something easy to cook, and I was looking forward to going for walks. Of course, my guitar was with me; I took it everywhere.

I was tired when I arrived, and as soon as I turned on the TV, I fell asleep. I woke up hungry in the middle of the night as I'd eaten nothing for dinner.

As I cooked my dinner, I shared my concerns with my Lord:

1. Do I stay, and why am I staying in Abilene town?

2. Should I accept the project?
3. Sarah? What about Sarah? Having a family one day?

What is God's will? Sometimes I found it complicated to figure it out, and then I would realize that I complicated things but the Lord's ways were full of wisdom and simple.

I had a lovely church, and the Eagles, and my friends, and a good job and a beautiful house. What more could I wish for?

The Lord had been patient and good to me, changing my heart and pouring blessings into my life. What more could I want?

But maybe it was time to move on: a new job would give me a new opportunity to achieve lots of projects. But what would moving entail? Living somewhere else, changing houses, churches, and friends? Yes, for sure. Was that what I really wanted?

I could work and travel; many people adopted that lifestyle if they did not have a family. A few months here and then back, and then on the road again. Interesting!

That would definitely change my relationship with God and my lifestyle, and I would possibly lose lots of friends. And there was also Sarah. Even if I did not want to admit it, she was there in my thoughts and my heart. She was one of my friends.

Sarah was just Sarah. So lovely and different, so simple and kind, and something made me enjoy her company and stay longer than I generally did with other women.

I remembered when she had that cold and I went to her house. I enjoyed being there with her and looking after her. And that, for me, was like a little wake-up call in my heart. Deep down in my heart were feelings taking root and desires springing up that I had long forgotten.

Me, going on a date? Me, having a family?

I started to laugh. The Lord would really have to have a sense of humour for me to have a wife and kids. It was something I might have desired when I was around 30, but not now that I had moved on a bit and was in my 40s.

Chapter 19

At Jesus' feet

I knew that the first thing I had to do was be truthful to myself. The most important thing was to invite the Lord into the situation and ask Him for wisdom. I loved sitting at Jesus' feet and listening. The Lord always revealed things to me and showed me ways that would never have crossed my mind.

His ways are higher than our ways. His will and timing are the best. Patience and perseverance in waiting on the Lord are key to taking the right steps, making the right choices.

The Lord is near to us in every circumstance and fire we go through. We just need to call upon His name, and His Spirit will lead us and comfort us.

I loved the worship song Call upon the Lord. I was calling now.

I had a very late breakfast and went for a walk. Behind the house was a huge wood with lots of footpaths where I often walked. I looked around and felt so much better. I felt as if a part of heaven was there with me, it was so peaceful and refreshing. Sometimes we want the easiest and quickest way out of a situation, but that is not necessarily the best for us. The Lord renews our strength like that of eagles when we wait upon Him and follow Him wholeheartedly.

Maybe it would be good to just leave and embark on a new career. Really? I stopped and looked at the birds. They were flying free with no worries, and the Lord was looking after them. He was looking after each one of them every day.

If I went to work with Peter Green, his company would be great. I'd worked with them before. I liked my job. I liked being in charge, with all kinds of challenges, but also being with the boys and getting my hands dirty. If I joined him on his latest project, I would have a break from Katie, the Eagles and, of course, Sarah.

I was running away, not trying to find a solution.

Since Sarah had joined the Eagles, it had been great. Her soft voice brought balance to the band. She started to sing most of the songs with me but sometimes also with Mark. I always encouraged other members of the band to sing, not just play instruments, so I was not the only one leading the singing. Mark had a beautiful voice, and Maria and Ruth also joined in sometimes.

Sarah, Sarah! What was wrong with Sarah? Nothing.

What was wrong with me, then?

I probably already knew what bothered me but had to dig deep into my heart for the unspoken truth. Even though I was a passionate person, I avoided dealing with those sorts of emotions. What the Lord told me was to go forward, you need to go backward. That was for me. I am sure the Lord was doing different things in other people's hearts. That was about me.

Years back, when I broke up with Olivia, it totally broke me down. I prayed and prayed for healing. We always need healing of our bodies, minds and hearts. But for me, the pain was so deep that I crashed. Once the Lord had brought me back onto the right track, I put up a barrier against falling in love, which was good. I was not the type to fall in love with every girl, but the barrier I put up was much higher than I realised

There was too much to think about and pray about, so I decided to stop. I chose to watch some movies I liked, Cheaper by the Dozen and Jackie Chan. I managed to cook dinner, had the TV on all evening and forgot about everything else.

After three hours, I heard the Lord speaking to my heart about peace and joy and love. I sat at his feet in quietness and listened.

"Going away and having a new job – would that bring you peace? Is that what you would you like to do?" the Lord asked me.

"I would like to plan and organize projects and travel; however, my heart would not have peace."

"Why?" the Lord asked me.

"Because I would miss my church and my friends, and my lovely Eagles and my music, and my sister and ..." I paused and took a big deep breath. "I would really miss Sarah."

I suddenly realized. I got it!

"I understand now, my Lord. If I go away, my heart will still be here."

The moment I acknowledged that, my heart was at peace.

The only way was to send Nick Palmer and to work with Peter on the project but not move there. I would just be away for a few days during the week when needed.

Then the Lord asked me, "What about Sarah?"

"That is a bit complicated and confusing, Lord."

"It is not, Daniel. I am the way, the truth and the life."

"Teach me, show me, reveal to me your will, my Lord."

The Lord whispered again to my heart, "Daniel, Daniel. You are afraid of a broken heart; you're afraid to trust again. Shine for the glory of God. Do not be afraid. I am with you."

"Shall I ask Sarah for a date?"

"What is your heart telling you?"

"My heart says yes, yes, my Lord."

"Follow your heart, Daniel. I am with you and I will guide you."

After sitting at Jesus' feet, I managed a very good night's sleep. On Tuesday morning, I had to start early. I was up doing my running at 6 am. It was just me and the birds at that hour. Who else would be awake then?

I was not sure whether I would go to work or not. After taking a shower, it was 7 am and I was back on the road.

* * *

Everyone at work was shocked to see him so early. It was only 8.30.

"Becky, I need to speak to Sarah Grant from Creative Ideas at 9:30, and before that, I need to speak to Peter Green from Green Houses."

"Good morning, Daniel," said Nick as he knocked on the door.

"Good morning, Nick! I need a list of all employees. Please come to my office at 10 o'clock for a serious conversation. We have work to do."

"All right, Daniel. You seem to be on the go. Anything else you need? By the way, everyone was quite startled to see you so early!" He grinned.

Daniel smiled. "I cannot remember the last time I was so early. No, I am fine. Just bring those lists and we can have a chat. Give me some time; I have some phone calls to make. Take a look at the Green Houses project." He handed him a folder of papers. At the same time, the phone rang and Nick left the room, closing the door behind him.

"Mr. Green on line 2, sir."

"Thank you, Becky. You are a star."

"Hey, hey Daniel. I was wondering when you would give me a call. Did you have a chance to look at my big project?"

"Yes, I did, and I think it's brilliant. I like all the plans and the way you have organized it. Good job, Peter."

"Thank you, Daniel. Now, the big question: are you coming to work with me in the field, or what do you have in mind?"

"I am saying yes and no. I can come for a few days now and then to coordinate, and you know how I am about coming and going. But I would like to send Nick Palmer, a nice young man, my right hand. I am quite happy here with my little company. And I can organize a team to work with your team and see what you think. That is the best I can do for you, Peter."

"Oh, Daniel, I am a bit disappointed. I was hoping to work directly with you for the entire period, but if you come now and then and supervise during the week, that would make me happy. What do you think about coming down on Thursday and we can have a face-to-face chat?"

"I will confirm through my secretary and let you know if I can come on Thursday."

"That would be great, Daniel. Looking forward to seeing you."

Things seemed to fall into place and Daniel was on the move. He had just hung up the phone when it rang again.

"Miss Sarah Grant, line 1, sir."

Daniel's heart started to beat a bit faster.

"Hello, Sarah. Daniel here. How are you?"

"I am fine, thank you. Looking forward to moving soon into my new house."

"Oh, yes, I almost forgot. You must be looking forward to that. I just gave you a short call to see if I could pop round for a chat maybe this evening? I know it is short notice."

"Let me see. Not sure. Wait a minute."

There was silence for a moment.

"I shall be home, and 6 pm will be fine."

"I will try my best for 6.30 as I will be out in the field with my boys."

"All right, Daniel, I will be waiting for you. See you later."

The rest of the day Daniel spent organising things with Nick Palmer, who was over the moon to be part of a big project.

Everything was going smoothly, and Daniel was not worried about time. He was pretty good at working under pressure and adapting.

He rushed home at 6 pm and hardly had time to shower and change. He didn't want to be late at Sarah's. But he was – it was already 7 pm.

"Good evening, Daniel. Working late?" Jane had opened the door.

"Yes, so sorry. You know me."

Jane welcomed him in. Daniel had a beautiful bouquet of flowers and as soon as he saw Sarah, he gave it to her.

"For you, Sarah."

She was very surprised and did not know how to react.

"Thank you!"

"Would you like something to eat?" asked Jane.

"I am starving, Jane. Yes, please."

Sarah put the flowers in a vase and he followed her.

"You haven't had time to eat yet?"

"No, Sarah, not yet. I have been on the go all day and had lots of things to sort out."

Jane looked after both of them. She put dinner on the table for Daniel and made cups of tea. However, she excused herself and went upstairs.

"How was your day, Sarah?"

"Very good, actually. One of my long-term clients wants to extend the project, and we managed to negotiate a three-year advertising contract."

Daniel was very relaxed. He always loved Jane's house; it was small and friendly. Sarah gradually became more confident and got into the conversation.

"There is a lovely conference next month, two days at church. Are you planning new worship songs?"

"It might be a good idea to organize some new songs for all of us. We can see what we agree on and practise them till then. Of course, we will still have some of our old, popular ones."

Jane came into the kitchen to pick up her tea and asked, "Did you not think about preaching? Jim keeps asking you..."

Daniel looked confused.

"Not sure I would be very good at it. I prefer my worship music, for now."

"I believe you would be quite good at preaching, Daniel."

He turned in surprise toward Sarah.

"You think so? Me, preaching? I will pray about it, but the last time I did, the Lord said no. It is not something I would jump into."

Half an hour later, Daniel and Sarah moved into the lounge.

He chose to sit on an armchair and she took the big couch.

He was looking and studying Sarah as he often did, which rather embarrassed her. He actually admired her.

"Sarah! I have been praying and thinking and asking the Lord. I was wondering if you would like to go out on a date with me."

He smiled and waited for her reaction.

She was shocked and did not move for a while. When their eyes met, she got shy again.

"Sarah, would you like to go out with me?"

"Yes, but... yes... but."

"Is it a yes?"

"I would love to go out with you; however, I would like to pray about it first."

Daniel was discouraged. He had expected a yes, maybe, or no. Was this a no or just him assuming a no as she'd asked for more time to pray?

"All right, Sarah. I'll wait to hear from you."

"Thank you, Daniel. I shall give you a call in the next couple of days."

He did not want to stay any longer, and in 10 minutes or so he apologised and left. At least he'd had to courage to ask her. He felt a bit flat, but finally, he was acting on his feelings.

Chapter 20

The boundaries of my heart – part 1

Sarah sat down on the couch. She was very quiet and her heart was beating fast. The TV was on, but she could not even hear it.

Jane came downstairs and asked, "Where is Daniel? Has he left already?"

"Yes, he has."

"Are you OK, Sarah?"

"Yes, I think so. Maybe I am a bit shocked!"

Jane looked concerned. "What is wrong? Problems with the new house?"

Sarah calmly replied, "No, no. Daniel asked me to go on a date with him."

"That's great, my child! That's good news. I hope you said yes. He is a lovely man and very dedicated to the Lord. Oh, I am so happy..."

Sarah stopped her. "I told him yes but also that I need a few days to pray. I am not sure."

"But why?"

"Jane, I am not sure I can do it. I am not sure I can go on a date. For me, it's very hard to trust someone in that way. Even though I would love to go out with him... It is complicated, Jane."

She stood up. "I'll pray about it. I'm going to bed now. I have to work early tomorrow."

* * *

Going to my room, I could not believe it: Daniel asked me out.

That was too much for me emotionally, and I did not want to think about it right now. I had to get used to the idea, which would take me some time.

I prayed about lots of things, then prayed specifically about me and Daniel.

I could not go out with him. Could I really trust again?

Deep down in my heart, I loved being with him. He was so much fun and always made me smile. His style of singing and his manner was so different from other people. He had been there for me lately and opened the door to music for me. He was patient with me when others were not. And yes, he was pretty good at listening to me. We'd met quite a lot lately in a variety of unexpected situations, which had given me a glimpse of who he was. He was a very passionate, kind soul, but full of joy and fire and love for the Lord. He was an amazing man.

And he asked me, the shy Sarah, for a date? Hmm...

On Thursday, I thought of calling Daniel and asking him to meet for a chat. But what would I tell him? That my heart had all kinds of boundaries and I was not sure how I could start a new relationship?

Becky, his secretary, told me that he was away and she was not sure when he would be back. That confused me more.

I struggled through the day and could hardly wait to get home. I found an excuse and went to bed early. My thoughts were all over the place; I spent time in prayer and then went back to bed. That is how I spent the night: a few hours asleep and a few hours awake.

Why was Daniel out of town? Was it because of me? Maybe he was busy. I spent the rest of my week wrestling with my worries and giving them to the Lord.

On Saturday, it was difficult to go to the church. Daniel was there, and I was not ready to meet him. I smiled at him and he seemed to be fine seeing me. He treated me the same and we sang together as if nothing had happened.

"You are very quiet today, Sarah?" said Thomas.

For me, that was normal, but possibly my friends noticed something was bothering me, and I did not like that.

After the service, Jane said, "Sarah, don't you think it might be a good idea to talk to Jim and Margaret? You did not sleep very well the past week, did you?"

"Yes, I think that's a brilliant idea."

As I was ready to leave, Margaret saw me and hurried to speak to me.

"Jim and I wondered if you wanted to join us for lunch?"

Wow, the Lord does know my heart, for sure.

"Yes, actually I wanted to speak with you."

Mark caught up with me and asked, "Are you not joining us at Rosie's today, Sarah?"

"Not today, I'm going to Jim and Margaret's." As I said this, my eyes met Daniel's. He smiled and turned around. He was leaving with the Eagles.

I felt so relieved to be going to Jim's house. I needed wise counsel and prayer and had felt stuck over the past days.

Jim and Margaret were always perfect hosts; they had lunch prepared and looked after me. Once I felt comfortable, we all sat in the lounge and started to chat. They were very good listeners and gave wise counsel.

"Sarah, so glad you could come. We prayed for you, and the Lord prompted us to ask you around."

"Yes, Jim and I spoke about how wonderfully you have come along in the Eagles. Everyone loves you, and we are so proud of you."

That was unexpected, as I had other thoughts in my mind.

I managed to say, "Thank you! I really love my friends at church."

A few tears escaped and I apologised.

"Are you all right, Sarah?" Margaret came and gave me a hug.

"Yes and no! I do not know. That's why I came to talk to you. I am waiting for an answer from the Lord, and I am confused and consumed. Or maybe I know the answer and do not know what to do."

I calmed down, and as I was not one for details, I said, "Daniel came around earlier in the week and asked me out on a date!"

Margaret and Jim smiled and looked at me with love.

"That's very good news. He is a lovely boy. And he has a love and a passion for the Lord. And what did you answer?"

"I said yes, but… I would pray about it. I am not sure I can do this. It is too much for me and it's hard to trust a man again. Long ago, I was in a relationship that went wrong."

Jim spoke up. "Have you spoken to Daniel since Tuesday?"

"No, I haven't. I really enjoy his company, and yes, I would like to go out with him. However, I am not the best at dealing with emotions, and I have no clue how to handle trust…"

Margaret and Jim interrupted me and prayed over me. They prayed for peace, wisdom and strength and asked the Lord to calm me down and show me His will in the matter.

"Let's take it one step at a time, Sarah. Why don't you meet Daniel and talk to him and tell him what you told us here? Speak the truth in love, as our Lord says. He probably does not even know what you are going through. You need to talk to him."

"True, Jim, I did say I would get back and talk to him."

"Why don't you go home today and relax? Trust the Lord and invite Him into your situation and He will bring you peace and joy.

He will give you wisdom and lead you step by step. The Lord is good and He knows your heart, Sarah."

Turning toward his wife, he said, "Margaret, what do you think if we ask Daniel and Sarah to come here tomorrow for lunch so they can have a chat here?"

"That is a good idea, Jim. Take one step at a time, child. Do not worry about tomorrow. Take a day at a time."

* * *

Back home, Sarah told Jane that Jim and Margaret were looking after her and Daniel.

"Such a blessing they are for our church, both of them. I am proud of you, girl. You have come a long way since I first met you."

Sunday came pretty quickly. The service was lovely and the worship songs inspiring and uplifting. Sarah sang three songs with Daniel. She struggled in her heart but managed to smile and hide the way she felt. She was anxious about the coming afternoon, and it was hard to focus on singing.

Daniel was pretty cool; at least, that is how he looked. How did he do it? He'd had to travel to meet with Peter, which had kept his mind off Sarah. No, he did not forget about her. She was still in his heart and his prayers. He did not think of calling her, but he did wonder whether she would come back with an answer. That yes was not much of a yes.

After the worship service, Jim approached him.

"Daniel, would you come to my house, please? I've asked Sarah to come as well. It will be nice for the two of you to talk. We spoke to her yesterday. What do you say?"

"All right, Jim. First I need to pick up some things from home for Mark, and I will be with you as soon as I can."

When he arrived at Jim's house, Sarah was already there. She was dressed in a red blouse and blue jeans. Everyone was waiting for him.

"How was your week, Daniel?" asked Margaret.

"I drove to see Peter Green and we talked about his new project."

He turned toward Sarah and explained. "Peter Green runs a large company, and he asked me and my company to join them in their new project of building a chain of houses in the West of England. We will be sending Nick Palmer and a team of my boys to work next to one of his best teams. The project is expected to stretch over a period of six months, and I did not want to be away that long. However, Nick was happy to cover one of the positions offered, and I will also help, travelling now and then during the week, coordinating. But I cannot miss my worship weekends, can I?" He smiled.

With big eyes, she asked, "So you were away for a few days this week?"

"Yes, I was away and just got back yesterday morning. Becky did tell me you tried to call me. You could have reached me on my cell phone, you know!"

Jim looked at his "son", marvelling at how bold and confident he had become and how he had grown closer to the Lord. The Lord was Daniel's Saviour, best friend, confidant, guide, healer and loving Father. The Lord brought him peace and joy, and His grace was showing in his life.

After lunch, Jim excused himself politely to help Margaret in the kitchen, not that she really needed help. Finally, Sarah and Daniel were alone.

"I was set up by Jim to meet you today, Sarah. So here I am."

She looked down shyly then slowly said, "Yes, I know. I spoke with them yesterday, and they advised me to speak to you, which I believe is right."

He looked at her and waited for her to continue.

"Daniel, you visited me on Tuesday evening and asked me for a date. I need to be honest with you. I was actually shocked that you would consider dating me. Maybe even honoured."

Daniel found that really funny. "I am just a man, Sarah!"

"You are a very dear friend and you are in a wonderful, close relationship with the Lord. I admire you. And you brought music back into my life!"

"Thank you. That makes my heart swell!" he teased.

She ignored his comments. "Lots of things happened to me in the past, but the Lord has been healing me. I was stuck in the past because of my parents; I did not want to admit they were 'not nice' to me to put it politely. After living with them for years, and then a broken relationship that I had, I ended up a bit weird, becoming shy and anxious. I find it hard to deal with certain emotions and trust people. I came a long way during the past year, even joining the Eagles team. That was a huge thing for me..."

Daniel interrupted her. "Sarah, you are not weird. You are a child of God with a beautiful, kind, gentle heart, and for me to sing with you and start knowing you is a blessing. I enjoy being with you."

"I would like to go out with you, Daniel. However, I find it very hard to deal with emotions, trust, anxiety..." She became unsettled in her chair.

Daniel did not seem concerned and calmed her down. It was something he had learned how to handle.

"Sarah, we will take a step at a time." He took her hand in his and looked into her eyes. She lifted her eyes and nodded. She was calm and not struggling.

"All right, Daniel."

The boundaries of her heart had started to melt. She felt brave and wanted to go out with him.

"Now, we will take it a day at a time. Sarah, the Lord is a good Father. He is with us and He will guide us and support us through his

Spirit. To be honest, I did not date for a long time after a relationship many years ago. I had such a broken heart that it took me years to heal. We always need healing, Sarah. We have both passed through some hard things in our lives, and I am sure the Lord will teach us how to trust and support each other, love each other. How to be faithful and truthful and have good communication with one another – grace."

"Yes, Daniel. We all need healing, and the Lord heals."

"We will walk this journey together, shall we?"

Chapter 21

The boundaries of my heart – part 2

On Tuesday, Daniel was supposed to meet Sarah for dinner on their first proper date. He was looking forward to it and had prayed about it but was a little nervous. Katie helped him to choose an outfit. He was not the type to wear formal shirts, but he had to admit he looked good in it.

"You will be fine, my little brother. I am so excited! You are going on a date. My baby is growing up!" Katie teased him.

"Stop it! You're embarrassing me."

"You will be fine. Look at you, such a young man. And you are 42. Going on a date at 42."

"Yes, and you got a bit ahead of me. You are already dating Jack. You might get married soon." He laughed.

"Yes! If you need any lessons, tell me. I can help you." She gave him a big hug.

He remembered how much fun he'd had with Katie. Such a dear sister and they were always there for each other.

He went to the office in his usual good mood and got on with his work. He had a number of appointments as he was trying to negotiate a new building contract.

He had a break for a few minutes and his mind went to Sarah. He was still smiling at the thought of going on a date. How much had changed in his life and how much he had changed! The Lord was definitely working in his heart.

His cell phone rang and it was Jim. He would never normally call at that hour.

"Hello, Daniel! Can we meet for lunch? I was thinking of coming to your canteen today. I really need to talk to you, and I wanted to make sure I caught you."

"Yes, of course, Jim. Seems important."

"I will be there in 20 minutes, son."

When he arrived, he did not seem as relaxed as Daniel and went straight to the point.

"Daniel, son, this letter is for you from Sarah!"

He took an envelope and gave it to him. He opened it and read the short handwritten message:

"Dear Daniel,

I'm sorry to leave without saying goodbye. I've decided to go back so I can go forward. I am away for a couple of weeks. I look forward to continuing with our relationship where we left it once I return. You are in my prayers.

Please do not call me or try to find me. I'll call you once I am back.

Talk to Jim – he will explain things to you.

In Christ,

Love,

Sarah"

"What's going on?" said Daniel.

Jim breathed deeply.

"To go forward, sometimes you need to go back, remember. She came by and dropped this letter for you. She has booked two weeks away, and she said she was not sure whether it might take her longer. I am afraid I cannot tell you where she is as she made me give my word."

"Did she?!"

"I contacted one of my friends, and she was very helpful. She will look after Sarah while she is there."

"It still does not make sense to me, Jim."

"Daniel," Jim touched his hand to get his full attention, "you must know a few things about her by now. However, what you do not know, maybe, is that she experienced some serious abuse in her life. Being mistreated caused her to create boundaries to her heart. Leaving is, in a way, a boundary, but the good part is she knows she needs to deal with those things before she will be able to date you and do many other things in her life as well. She needs to discover who she is, her identity in Christ. Many people put up boundaries or barriers when they face new challenges. Some are good and sensible, but others are just to protect themselves when they are afraid to try again after failing. Her heart has a lot of boundaries and barriers."

"Jim, I am not very happy. We were supposed to go out on our first date tonight and I feel kind of stood up. I'm not doing very well, am I?"

"Daniel, I understand how you feel, hurt and rejected and as if she said no. But she did not say no. The Lord is looking after her heart and also yours. Remember that you also went through some things and have been healed. You should show grace."

This was too much for Daniel.

"Listen, Jim, I am busy at work. I will have to go home and meditate on it and pray. At this point, I even regret asking her to go out with me. Maybe it really was too much for her. When we met at your house, she seemed fine to me. We spoke about taking it a step at a time."

"Son, please do not get upset. The best you can do is pray and forgive and stand next to her and show grace. Do you not think that maybe it's a test from the Lord for both of you? If you cannot stand next to each other now, how will you last later?"

"But I want to help her. I do want to talk to her. I do want to stand next to her." He stood up, ready to go.

"Please sit down, son."

"No, I cannot let her go like this. She is running away. I want to help her and stand by her. I really love Sarah, Jim!"

Jim looked calmly at the young man.

"Daniel, you must know that Sarah loves you too. Otherwise, she would not have done what she is doing, even if it does not make sense."

Daniel felt too confused and hurt to listen much.

"Daniel, if it was you going through what she is going through now, what would you have done? Would you have been able to enter into a relationship if you felt you still had some loose ends?"

He sat down, sad and discouraged.

"I would have sorted my life out first, then got into a relationship."

"Now, let the Lord sort things out. It might be confusing, but Margaret and I and Jane are praying for Sarah. No one else knows the story. You are praying, and you need to trust the Lord. You did the right thing and followed your heart. You fell in love with each other. It is beautiful. You make such a wonderful couple. You turned her world upside down and she needs time."

Daniel shook his head unhappily.

"Why does she not want me to speak to her or even know where she is?"

"Would you not have gone after her?"

He laughed. "I would probably have driven there right now to bring her back." Looking at the clock, he stood up. "Jim, you are more than welcome to stay. I have to leave in 10 minutes. I need to go and see the boys and there is a delivery on the site as well."

"No problem, Daniel. But can you please promise you will not call her?"

"I am sorry Jim, but I cannot promise anything."

* * *

He was home by 8.00 and wanted a quiet evening. He ate something simple and decided to stop wrestling with the Lord. Maybe he was afraid of losing her. Yes, afraid.

Probably, she would remain in her own castle and stay shy and quiet. Yes, that's what would probably happen at the end of the two weeks.

Sarah was already in the little cottage she had rented, an hour's drive away. She had decided at the last moment. How Daniel would react she was not sure, but she imagined him being upset and angry with her.

"I have to do it, Jim. I have to!" She remembered the words she had said to Jim before she left.

A knock at the door woke her up.

"Hello, I am Dennise. Jim told me you'd arrived."

Dennise was an old friend of Jim and Margaret's. She only came to say hello and give Sarah her phone number. She invited her to lunch the following day, and Sarah accepted, although she was not in the mood to go out. For some reason, she felt like crying and very anxious.

The cottage was cosy, but she did not notice anything around her. She made herself something to eat and cuddled on the couch under a blanket.

"How can I go on? How?" she asked the Lord.

Why are you sad? she heard the Lord saying.

She could not pray but she wanted to empty her heart.

Memories from her childhood came and stories and events, and one by one she gave them to Jesus. She cried about everything, and by the time she looked at the clock, three hours had passed.

Some people cannot do this, just forgive and move on. For her, it was different. She wanted to go into the past and wanted to know and let go.

She fell asleep on the couch and woke up the next morning feeling that something was different. She had not even used the bedroom. She spent all night on the couch.

Her phone rang and Jane was on the other end.

"Hello, Sarah. How are you, my child?"

"I am fine, Jane, fine. I had a good long night's sleep. And I am meeting Dennise for lunch."

"Good, good. Margaret spoke to her. She is there for you if you need anything."

The lunch was pleasant, and then she decided to take a walk by the sea. The waves were much like her heart, like a storm. She sat down on the rocks, not realizing it was already 5 in the evening. She felt cold and lonely. She cried and cried until, suddenly, she felt a burden being lifted from her shoulders. At that moment, she stood up, took off a necklace she was wearing and looked at it. It brought back a memory.

A group of young children came walking along the beach. As they approached, she walked towards them, smiled and said, "I would like you to have this necklace!" She gave it to a girl with long hair.

They all looked at her, surprised, but the girl took it and thanked her.

From that moment, she felt she could move on and be in present, not stuck in the past. She went home feeling that all the horrible memories were now at Jesus' feet and she was free indeed.

The next days she spent relaxing, visiting the area and meeting with Dennise, who became very dear to her. She was an elderly lady who, like Jane, was dedicated to serving the Lord.

Sarah shared with her some things from her past, and she was a very good listener. She would reply with Bible verses and speak courage and love.

"How is your life now, Sarah?" she asked.

"Now, I'm not sure. Daniel – it's because of Daniel I am here. Not because I really wanted to be."

Dennise looked at her.

"Who is Daniel? You haven't spoken about him before."

Sarah smiled, thinking of him.

"Tall, handsome, blue eyes, messy blondish hair. Beautiful voice! Passionate for the Lord, kind and patient, but stubborn, never gives up. Full of joy and always pushing me for more. Never know what to expect with him and ..."

Dennise looked at her as she stopped, with her mind far away.

"And I fell in love with him."

Dennise smiled as she brought her a cup of tea.

"That is good, is it not?"

"Dennise, I came here because he asked me for a date. I said yes and no and finally we talked and... I had to walk back into my past to be able to go forward..."

Then Sarah explained all her anxiety and also the boundaries of her heart.   When she'd finished, Dennise gave her a hug.

"Now he might be upset with me and not want to date me anymore. But I had to sort out that part of my heart. I had to..."

"I am sure it will be all right, Sarah. God is good."

The first week passed quickly, but for Daniel, time moved slowly. He felt down and confused and it took him days to wrestle with it in prayer and surrender his thoughts to the Lord. Slowly the confusion disappeared and he found peace in the presence of the Saviour. The Lord had him in the palm of his hand, a loving Father who always looked after Him.

Daniel decided to join a team from the church that went to the hospital to pray and spend time with those who were asking for support and someone to speak or pray with them. He chose to go and help to avoid being home and getting lost in his thoughts.

On Saturday morning after the worship service, Daniel went straight home and had a quiet afternoon as Katie was out with the girls. He *did* miss Sarah and was wondering how she was. Worship without her was lonely for him, but he did a good job and his friends were good enough not to tease him about Sarah not being there. He managed to keep his word and not call her, but he often looked at his phone and had to change his mind. Jim was proud of him, but he was not sure he was proud of himself.

Around 4 pm, when he was on the couch playing his guitar, he heard a knock at the door. He went to open it, thinking that Katie had probably forgotten something. He saw someone he did not expect.

"Sarah!"

"Hello, Daniel! How are you?

"Hello, yes. You here? Now? I thought you were supposed to come back next week."

He wanted to give her a hug but waited to hear what she had to say.

"I've kept my word – I came back. I thought you might want to go out for dinner and we could have a proper conversation as you probably have lots of questions."

It was so unexpected, he forgot he was upset with her.

"All right, Sarah. We can go. Give me five minutes to change."

On the way into the town centre, there was a deep silence in the car. Daniel was not in the mood for conversation, unwilling to become more confused than he already was.

Sarah looked beautiful in a lovely pink dress and cardigan. She looked like a flower that had opened.

Daniel suggested a nice little Italian restaurant where they found a table at the back, quite romantic.

They looked at the menu but he was not much interested in food. However, they ordered a starter to share and a selection of ham and cold meat.

"You came back earlier than I expected, Sarah?" Daniel decided to start the conversation and he was eager to hear her story.

She raised her head. She was still shy but something was different in her behaviour.

"Daniel, I did leave quite unexpectedly and I am sorry!"

"You really upset me, you know that?"

She looked at me again as if begging me.

"I'm always upsetting you lately, aren't I?"

He smiled and looked at her with admiration.

"Daniel, I am sorry, I did not mean to hurt you. I had to spend a few days with the Lord and be away so I would have a clear mind. When you came to my house and asked me for a date, that blew my mind. It was too much for me and I felt unprepared; I felt confused, I felt happy. I had to go somewhere quiet so I could speak to the Lord and go back into the past so I could go forward. Meeting at Jim and Margaret's was good, but some things I had to do alone, not with you or anyone else. Just me and the Lord. Does it make sense?"

"Did you find your peace, Sarah?"

"Yes, I did, Daniel."

He looked at his plate and was quiet for a moment.

"Sarah, would you like to finally go out with me?" he asked, laughing.

"Yes, Daniel, and I promise I won't run away again."

"Good. So are we taking one step at a time?"

"Yes, we are taking one step at a time."

Daniel took a deep breath.

"Sarah, I am in love with you and I want to be with you."

She put her head down and whispered, "And Daniel, I am in love with you too."

They looked into each other's eyes and smiled. For the first time, they seemed to be on the same level – love.

"Listen, Sarah, I know you are struggling with trust and you have been through some hard times. There will be days when it won't be easy for you or for me. I want us to develop trust in each other and let the Lord guide us. And remember I am here for you. Please do not run away."

She felt so blessed; he was a very sweet man.

"Daniel, you are very patient. How do you do it?"

"Sarah, it is a journey and I am still getting there, but I made a decision to stand by you no matter what and I will keep my word. I am here and not leaving. I am not perfect, but I am me, Daniel. I will make you smile, I will challenge you and hurt you, I will say I am sorry. But I am here. I will laugh with you and stand by you. I am here. And I have no intention of leaving."

Tears trickled down her face.

He stroked her cheek and smiled.

"Hey, girl, let's talk about something else. We are on our first date, aren't we?"

"Yes, yes, of course. I was wondering about the coming conference – maybe we can choose some songs together."

Daniel looked at her, surprised by her boldness.

"But it might be a bit too much for me; maybe I could sing two songs. What do you think?"

"Sarah, you are adorable when you get shy! You are so beautiful."

"Don't tease me. I am serious. It will be too much for me as there will be lots of people in the room."

"Sorry, I just think you are so sweet. We will choose a few songs and see at practice how you handle it. Please sing with me. What would I do without you, sing with Mark? He usual sings alone or with Ruth sometimes."

"We'll see at the practice how we get along. You will be there, won't you?"

"Listen, Sarah, I will be there, but you need to be confident and trust the Lord. Stand on your own two feet. You are there for the Lord. However, we are a pretty good team."

"Yes, you are right, we are a very nice team."

"Oh, can you imagine what the Eagles will say when they hear we are dating?"

"I am sure they will all be very happy for us. People have been talking about our dating for some time. Sometimes others see things we do not."

As they were leaving, Daniel took her gently by the hand. Sarah had very cold little hands and his were so warm. She walked close to him and leaned on his shoulder.

"I'm getting a bit cold."

"It is getting late and we have worship tomorrow. Where is your car?"

"It is at your house!"

"All right, then we'll go to my house."

There was silence in the car until Sarah said, "Daniel, thank you very much for this evening. It was very..."

"Unexpected..."

"Better than I expected. I was afraid you had already forgotten about me."

Parking the car on the driveway, Daniel said softly, "I cannot forget your beautiful eyes and lovely smile. I've got myself a pretty beautiful girlfriend."

"I must go. I am getting really cold and I forgot my coat."

Daniel jumped out of the car. "Wait a minute."

In no time, he brought her one of his jackets.

"You can take this one. It is very warm, one of my favourites," and he helped her put it on.

"Thank you, again, and goodnight, Daniel."

He leaned toward her and kissed her on the cheek. He held her tight for a while and closed his eyes. She was so much in his heart. Love, love and love.

She did not struggle but she took a deep breath as she started to get anxious.

"What do you think if we pop around to Jim's house tomorrow, after the service? I am sure they would be happy to see us. Would you like me to pick you up? I can pick Jane up too."

"Yes, let's give it a go. Maybe I can move one more step, hey Daniel? What do you think?"

It was a beautiful Sunday and everyone was there. When the main doors opened, Daniel entered with Sarah and they were holding hands. They looked beautiful together. Jane was walking in front of them, feeling very happy. It seemed like the best day of her life.

"Our Daniel is growing up!" said Mark as he came in from a side door. "Oh, you got yourself a girlfriend."

Sarah felt shy and smiled. Daniel laughed and replied, "Not, any one. It's my Sarah!"

Ruth and a few others came around the couple and were equally happy. However, Sarah felt it was too much all at once.

Daniel noticed and smoothly made a way for them to go behind the stage so they could get ready for the worship songs and they usually had a time of prayer.

"Thank you, Daniel. Uh, it got a bit much for me."

All the band was there, and after they had prayed, Daniel said, "You weren't at the practice yesterday. Do you want to sing at the back, Sarah, as my echo or would you prefer to have a miss? You know the majority of the songs, but Mark is playing a new song. Here is the list for today. I am singing two new songs."

"What do you think, Daniel?"

"I believe you can sing echo to the songs you know, and I will have to sing those two new songs with Ruth. I practised with Ruth. Is that alright?"

"Yes, we are all fine with that."

"I can't believe it, Daniel! You two are dating."

Daniel cut Thomas short. "We can talk more later... Now it's worship. Let's praise the Lord..."

After the service, they went to Jim's house and Margaret opened the door. She smiled, seeing Daniel holding Sarah's hand.

"Come in, come in. Jim and I have organized a very nice lunch. It is different: we ordered Chinese takeaway!"

Sarah looked surprised and whispered, "I didn't know they even ate Chinese."

Daniel whispered, "They don't; they are doing it for us."

Jim was already in the lounge and the food had just been delivered.

"Sit down, sit down. How are you?"

"We are fine, thank you."

Daniel and Sarah sat on one couch and Jim and Margaret faced them on the other.

"Shall we give thanks for the food and all God's blessings? Daniel, would you like to lead us in prayer?"

Daniel was surprised as Jim always said the prayer.

"Our Lord God and Father, thank you for your love, for family and friends, and for your mercy and grace. Thank you for this food. Bless us throughout the day as we spend time with each other. Amen."

"Jim, Margaret, you have been my spiritual parents and you keep looking after me. I really love you."

This brought tears to Jim's eyes.

"Sarah and I had a good conversation yesterday evening, and she finally said yes to going out with me. And she promised not to run away." He looked at her and she smiled.

"So we are dating, as of yesterday. We wanted you to be one of the first to know. My parents will find out later today. Katie and Jane know."

Margaret and Jim came and gave each of them a hug.

"I am more than happy, Daniel, and I believe that the entire church knows," said Jim, laughing. "Sarah, Daniel, you are a beautiful couple and the Lord is with you. Stay close to the Lord and He will never leave you nor forsake you," and he spoke a blessing over them.

* * *

It was a beautiful summer's day. Almost two years had passed since Sarah and Daniel started dating. Jim stood up and spoke.

"Today, we join together Daniel and Sarah in marriage. It is such a joy for me and for all of us. We celebrate with you and rejoice. When the Lord brings two people together, it is beautiful, and the Holy Spirit works amazing things.

"His grace is always with us, and His grace has brought Daniel and Sarah into beautiful unity. The Lord is good and will help you walk this journey of love.

Daniel stood up and read his vows to Sarah:

"Sarah, my beautiful wife,

Today I stand here as your husband.

I am not perfect, it is true.

I will smile with you; I will cry with you.

I will hurt you and

I will say I am sorry.

I will make you laugh.

I will be faithful and trustworthy.

I am here with you.

I will hold you tight and never let you go.

I will always love you!"

* * *

1 Corinthians 13:4-8

Love is patient and kind; love does not envy or boast; it is not arrogant or rude. It does not insist on its own way; it is not irritable or resentful; it does not rejoice at wrongdoing, but rejoices with the truth. Love bears all things, believes all things, hopes all things, endures all things. Love never ends.

The End

Bible Verse References
English Standard Version – ESV Bible

Chapter 1 – Memories

John 3:16
For God so loved the world that he gave his only Son, that whoever believes in him should not perish but have eternal life.

Ephesians 2:8-9
For by grace you have been saved through faith. And this is not your own doing; it is the gift of God, not a result of works, so that no one may boast.

Romans 15:13
May the God of hope fill you with all joy and peace in believing, so that by the power of the Holy Spirit you may abound in hope.

Romans 5:3-4
More than that, we rejoice in our sufferings, knowing that suffering produces endurance, and endurance produces character, and character produces hope...

1 Peter 5:7
Casting all your anxieties on him, because he cares for you.

John 14:27
Peace I leave with you; my peace I give to you. Not as the world gives do I give to you. Let not your hearts be troubled, neither let them be afraid.

Matthew 6:26
Look at the birds of the air: they neither sow nor reap nor gather into barns, and yet your heavenly Father feeds them. Are you not of more value than they?

Jeremiah 31:3
The Lord appeared to him from far away. I have loved you with an everlasting love; therefore I have continued my faithfulness to you.

Proverbs 3:5-6
Trust in the Lord with all your heart, and do not lean on your own understanding. In all your ways acknowledge him, and he will make straight your paths.

James 4:7
Submit yourselves therefore to God. Resist the devil, and he will flee from you.

Philippians 4:6
Do not be anxious about anything, but in everything by prayer and supplication with thanksgiving let your requests be made known to God.

Psalm 4:8
In peace I will both lie down and sleep; for you alone, O Lord, make me dwell in safety.

Chapter 2 – First Step

Psalm 29:2
Ascribe to the Lord the glory due his name; worship the Lord in the splendor of holiness.

Isaiah 12:5
Sing praises to the Lord, for he has done gloriously; let this be made known in all the earth.

Galatians 2:20

I have been crucified with Christ. It is no longer I who live, but Christ who lives in me. And the life I now live in the flesh I live by faith in the Son of God, who loved me and gave himself for me.

Hebrews 13:8

Jesus Christ is the same yesterday and today and forever.

Ephesians 2:8-9

For by grace you have been saved through faith. And this is not your own doing; it is the gift of God, not a result of works, so that no one may boast.

Jeremiah 29:11

For I know the plans I have for you, declares the Lord, plans for welfare and not for evil, to give you a future and a hope.

John 8:12

Again Jesus spoke to them, saying, "I am the light of the world. Whoever follows me will not walk in darkness, but will have the light of life."

John 3:16

For God so loved the world that he gave his only Son, that whoever believes in him should not perish but have eternal life.

Romans 14:17

For the kingdom of God is not a matter of eating and drinking but of righteousness and peace and joy in the Holy Spirit.

James 1:2-3

Count it all joy, my brothers, when you meet trials of various kinds, for you know that the testing of your faith produces steadfastness.

Chapter 3 – Moving on

1 John 4:6
We are from God. Whoever knows God listens to us; whoever is not from God does not listen to us. By this we know the Spirit of truth and the spirit of error.

Psalm 116:1-2
I love the Lord because he has heard my voice and my pleas for mercy. Because he inclined his ear to me, therefore I will call on him as long as I live.

Ephesians 1:18-19
Having the eyes of your hearts enlightened, that you may know what is the hope to which he has called you, what are the riches of his glorious inheritance in the saints, and what is the immeasurable greatness of his power toward us who believe, according to the working of his great might

John 16:33
I have said these things to you, that in me you may have peace. In the world you will have tribulation. But take heart; I have overcome the world.

Psalm 147:3
He heals the brokenhearted and binds up their wounds.

Hebrews 11:6
And without faith it is impossible to please him, for whoever would draw near to God must believe that he exists and that he rewards those who seek him.

Jeremiah 29:13
You will seek me and find me, when you seek me with all your heart.

3 John 1:2
Beloved, I pray that all may go well with you and that you may be in good health, as it goes well with your soul.

Isaiah 41:10
Fear not, for I am with you; be not dismayed, for I am your God; I will strengthen you, I will help you, I will uphold you with my righteous right hand.

Chapter 4 – Help me, please!

Psalm 54:4
Behold, God is my helper; the Lord is the upholder of my life.

Psalm 34:17
When the righteous cry for help, the Lord hears and delivers them out of all their troubles.

Proverbs 28:1
The wicked flee when no one pursues, but the righteous are bold as a lion.

Hebrews 13:6
So we can confidently say, "The Lord is my helper; I will not fear; what can man do to me?"

Romans 8:28
And we know that for those who love God all things work together for good, for those who are called according to his purpose.

Psalm 34:19
Many are the afflictions of the righteous, but the Lord delivers him out of them all.

Philippians 2:13
For it is God who works in you, both to will and to work for his good pleasure.

1 Peter 4:10
As each has received a gift, use it to serve one another, as good stewards of God's varied grace:

James 1:17
Every good gift and every perfect gift is from above, coming down from the Father of lights with whom there is no variation or shadow due to change.

Isaiah 41:10
Fear not, for I am with you; be not dismayed, for I am your God; I will strengthen you, I will help you, I will uphold you with my righteous right hand.

Acts 2:38
And Peter said to them, "Repent and be baptized every one of you in the name of Jesus Christ for the forgiveness of your sins, and you will receive the gift of the Holy Spirit. For the promise is for you and for your children and for all who are far off, everyone whom the Lord our God calls to himself.

Romans 8:14
For all who are led by the Spirit of God are sons of God.

Galatians 3:26
For in Christ Jesus you are all sons of God, through faith.

John 3:5-6
Jesus answered, "Truly, truly, I say to you, unless one is born of water and the Spirit, he cannot enter the kingdom of God. That which is born of the flesh is flesh, and that which is born of the Spirit is spirit.

Chapter 5 – My home?

Philippians 1:6
And I am sure of this, that he who began a good work in you will bring it to completion at the day of Jesus Christ.

2 Timothy 3:16-17
All Scripture is breathed out by God and profitable for teaching, for reproof, for correction, and for training in righteousness, that the man of God may be competent, equipped for every good work.

Romans 12:2
Do not be conformed to this world, but be transformed by the renewal of your mind, that by testing you may discern what is the will of God, what is good and acceptable and perfect.

John 4:24
God is spirit, and those who worship him must worship in spirit and truth.

Isaiah 12:5
Sing praises to the Lord, for he has done gloriously; let this be made known in all the earth.

Psalm 29:2
Ascribe to the Lord the glory due his name; worship the Lord in the splendor of holiness.

James 4:6
But he gives more grace. Therefore it says, "God opposes the proud, but gives grace to the humble."

2 Corinthians 5:17
Therefore, if anyone is in Christ, he is a new creation. The old has passed away; behold, the new has come.

1 Peter 2:9
But you are a chosen race, a royal priesthood, a holy nation, a people for his own possession, that you may proclaim the excellencies of him who called you out of darkness into his marvelous light.

Galatians 3:26
For in Christ Jesus you are all sons of God, through faith.

Isaiah 61:3
To grant to those who mourn in Zion— to give them a beautiful headdress instead of ashes, the oil of gladness instead of mourning, the garment of praise instead of a faint spirit; that they may be called oaks of righteousness, the planting of the Lord, that he may be glorified.

Matthew 6:14-15
For if you forgive others their trespasses, your heavenly Father will also forgive you, but if you do not forgive others their trespasses, neither will your Father forgive your trespasses.

Mark 11:25
And whenever you stand praying, forgive, if you have anything against anyone, so that your Father also who is in heaven may forgive you your trespasses.

Ephesians 4:32
Be kind to one another, tenderhearted, forgiving one another, as God in Christ forgave you.

John 14:6
Jesus said to him, "I am the way, and the truth, and the life. No one comes to the Father except through me.

John 1:16
And from his fullness we have all received grace upon grace.

Chapter 6 – One more step

1 John 1:9
If we confess our sins, he is faithful and just to forgive us our sins and to cleanse us from all unrighteousness.

Colossians 3:15
And let the peace of Christ rule in your hearts, to which indeed you were called in one body. And be thankful.

2 Thessalonians 3:16
Now may the Lord of peace himself give you peace at all times in every way. The Lord be with you all.

Galatians 6:2
Bear one another's burdens, and so fulfill the law of Christ.

Psalm 55:22
Cast your burden on the Lord, and he will sustain you; he will never permit the righteous to be moved.

Philippians 4:6-7
Do not be anxious about anything, but in everything by prayer and supplication with thanksgiving let your requests be made known to God. And the peace of God, which surpasses all understanding, will guard your hearts and your minds in Christ Jesus.

Psalm 99:3
Let them praise your great and awesome name! Holy is he!

Psalm 69:30
I will praise the name of God with a song; I will magnify him with thanksgiving.

Philippians 4:4
Rejoice in the Lord always; again I will say, Rejoice.

Psalm 118:24
This is the day that the Lord has made; let us rejoice and be glad in it.

Romans 15:13
May the God of hope fill you with all joy and peace in believing, so that by the power of the Holy Spirit you may abound in hope.

Psalm 100:1-2
A Psalm for giving thanks. Make a joyful noise to the Lord, all the earth! Serve the Lord with gladness! Come into his presence with singing!

Psalm 95:1-2
Oh come, let us sing to the Lord; let us make a joyful noise to the rock of our salvation! Let us come into his presence with thanksgiving; let us make a joyful noise to him with songs of praise!

Ephesians 5:19
Addressing one another in psalms and hymns and spiritual songs, singing and making melody to the Lord with your heart,

Psalm 147:1
Praise the Lord! For it is good to sing praises to our God; for it is pleasant, and a song of praise is fitting.

Philippians 4:6-7
Do not be anxious about anything, but in everything by prayer and supplication with thanksgiving let your requests be made known to God. And the peace of God, which surpasses all understanding, will guard your hearts and your minds in Christ Jesus.

1 Peter 5:7
Casting all your anxieties on him, because he cares for you.

Chapter 7 – The Help Team

John 3:16-17

"For God so loved the world, that he gave his only Son, that whoever believes in him should not perish but have eternal life. For God did not send his Son into the world to condemn the world, but in order that the world might be saved through him.

Proverbs 18:24

A man of many companions may come to ruin, but there is a friend who sticks closer than a brother.

Proverbs 17:17

A friend loves at all times, and a brother is born for adversity.

Proverbs 13:20

Whoever walks with the wise becomes wise, but the companion of fools will suffer harm.

Ephesians 6:18

Praying at all times in the Spirit, with all prayer and supplication. To that end keep alert with all perseverance, making supplication for all the saints

1 Thessalonians 5:15-17

See that no one repays anyone evil for evil, but always seek to do good to one another and to everyone. Rejoice always, pray without ceasing,

Colossians 4:2

Continue steadfastly in prayer, being watchful in it with thanksgiving.

Proverbs 1:7

The fear of the Lord is the beginning of knowledge; fools despise wisdom and instruction.

Proverbs 19:20
Listen to advice and accept instruction, that you may gain wisdom in the future.

James 3:17
But the wisdom from above is first pure, then peaceable, gentle, open to reason, full of mercy and good fruits, impartial and sincere.

Psalm 111:10
The fear of the Lord is the beginning of wisdom; all those who practice it have a good understanding. His praise endures forever!

Psalm 119:105
Your word is a lamp to my feet and a light to my path.

Psalm 119:130
The unfolding of your words gives light; it imparts understanding to the simple.

Psalm 27:14
Wait for the Lord; be strong, and let your heart take courage; wait for the Lord!

Psalm 31:24
Be strong, and let your heart take courage, all you who wait for the Lord!

Philippians 4:13
I can do all things through him who strengthens me.

Chapter 8 – Katie

Matthew 6:33-35
But seek first the kingdom of God and his righteousness, and all these things will be added to you. "Therefore do not be anxious about tomorrow, for tomorrow will be anxious for itself. Sufficient for the day is its own trouble.

Psalm 34:4
I sought the Lord, and he answered me and delivered me from all my fears.

Psalm 23:1-4
A Psalm of David. The Lord is my shepherd; I shall not want. He makes me lie down in green pastures. He leads me beside still waters. He restores my soul. He leads me in paths of righteousness for his name's sake. Even though I walk through the valley of the shadow of death, I will fear no evil, for you are with me; your rod and your staff, they comfort me.

1 Peter 5:7
Casting all your anxieties on him, because he cares for you.

Philippians 4:6-7
Do not be anxious about anything, but in everything by prayer and supplication with thanksgiving let your requests be made known to God. And the peace of God, which surpasses all understanding, will guard your hearts and your minds in Christ Jesus.

Philippians 4:13
I can do all things through him who strengthens me.

Matthew 6:14-15
For if you forgive others their trespasses, your heavenly Father will also forgive you, but if you do not forgive others their trespasses, neither will your Father forgive your trespasses.

Ephesians 4:32
Be kind to one another, tenderhearted, forgiving one another, as God in Christ forgave you.

Ephesians 1:7-9
In him we have redemption through his blood, the forgiveness of our trespasses, according to the riches of his grace, which he lavished

upon us, in all wisdom and insight making known to us the mystery of his will, according to his purpose, which he set forth in Christ.

Romans 8:18

For I consider that the sufferings of this present time are not worth comparing with the glory that is to be revealed to us.

Romans 5:3-5

More than that, we rejoice in our sufferings, knowing that suffering produces endurance, and endurance produces character, and character produces hope, and hope does not put us to shame, because God's love has been poured into our hearts through the Holy Spirit who has been given to us.

Proverbs 15:1

A soft answer turns away wrath, but a harsh word stirs up anger.

John 14:27

Peace I leave with you; my peace I give to you. Not as the world gives do I give to you. Let not your hearts be troubled, neither let them be afraid.

1 Peter 5:6-7

Humble yourselves, therefore, under the mighty hand of God so that at the proper time he may exalt you, casting all your anxieties on him, because he cares for you.

Chapter 9 – Changing

Joshua 1:8

This Book of the Law shall not depart from your mouth, but you shall meditate on it day and night, so that you may be careful to do according to all that is written in it. For then you will make your way prosperous, and then you will have good success.

Psalm 1:1-6

Blessed is the man who walks not in the counsel of the wicked, nor stands in the way of sinners, nor sits in the seat of scoffers; but his delight is in the law of the Lord, and on his law he meditates day and night.

Philippians 4:8

Finally, brothers, whatever is true, whatever is honorable, whatever is just, whatever is pure, whatever is lovely, whatever is commendable, if there is any excellence, if there is anything worthy of praise, think about these things.

Psalm 19:14

Let the words of my mouth and the meditation of my heart be acceptable in your sight, O Lord, my rock and my redeemer.

Mark 11:24

Therefore I tell you, whatever you ask in prayer, believe that you have received it, and it will be yours.

Matthew 6:6

But when you pray, go into your room and shut the door and pray to your Father who is in secret. And your Father who sees in secret will reward you.

Luke 11:9

And I tell you, ask, and it will be given to you; seek, and you will find; knock, and it will be opened to you.

Romans 8:26

Likewise the Spirit helps us in our weakness. For we do not know what to pray for as we ought, but the Spirit himself intercedes for us with groanings too deep for words.

Psalm 54:4
Behold, God is my helper; the Lord is the upholder of my life.

Psalm 28:7
The Lord is my strength and my shield; in him my heart trusts, and I am helped; my heart exults, and with my song I give thanks to him.

1 Timothy 5:8
But if anyone does not provide for his relatives, and especially for members of his household, he has denied the faith and is worse than an unbeliever.

1 Peter 3:8
Finally, all of you, have unity of mind, sympathy, brotherly love, a tender heart, and a humble mind.

Acts 20:35
In all things I have shown you that by working hard in this way we must help the weak and remember the words of the Lord Jesus, how he himself said, 'It is more blessed to give than to receive.'

Romans 12:2
Do not be conformed to this world, but be transformed by the renewal of your mind, that by testing you may discern what is the will of God, what is good and acceptable and perfect.

Chapter 10 – Broken heart – heal me, Lord

John 14:6
Jesus said to him, "I am the way, and the truth, and the life. No one comes to the Father except through me. If you had known me, you would have known my Father also. From now on you do know him and have seen him."

1 Corinthians 6:19-20
Or do you not know that your body is a temple of the Holy Spirit within you, whom you have from God? You are not your own, for you were bought with a price. So glorify God in your body.

Psalm 34:18
The Lord is near to the brokenhearted and saves the crushed in spirit.

Psalm 51:17
The sacrifices of God are a broken spirit; a broken and contrite heart, O God, you will not despise.

2 Corinthians 12:9
But he said to me, "My grace is sufficient for you, for my power is made perfect in weakness." Therefore I will boast all the more gladly of my weaknesses, so that the power of Christ may rest upon me.

Matthew 11:28-30
Come to me, all who labor and are heavy laden, and I will give you rest. Take my yoke upon you, and learn from me, for I am gentle and lowly in heart, and you will find rest for your souls. For my yoke is easy, and my burden is light."

Jeremiah 17:14
Heal me, O Lord, and I shall be healed; save me, and I shall be saved, for you are my praise.

Isaiah 53:5
But he was wounded for our transgressions; he was crushed for our iniquities; upon him was the chastisement that brought us peace, and with his stripes we are healed.

Isaiah 41:10
Fear not, for I am with you; be not dismayed, for I am your God; I will strengthen you, I will help you, I will uphold you with my righteous right hand.

2 Timothy 1:7
For God gave us a spirit not of fear but of power and love and self-control.

1 Corinthians 16:13
Be watchful, stand firm in the faith, act like men, be strong.

John 15:13
Greater love has no one than this, that someone lay down his life for his friends.

1 Thessalonians 5:11
Therefore encourage one another and build one another up, just as you are doing.

1 John 4:7
Beloved, let us love one another, for love is from God, and whoever loves has been born of God and knows God.

Chapter 11 – Hannah

Hebrews 4:12
For the word of God is living and active, sharper than any two-edged sword, piercing to the division of soul and of spirit, of joints and of marrow, and discerning the thoughts and intentions of the heart.

Ephesians 5:15
Look carefully then how you walk, not as unwise but as wise,

Galatians 5:22-23
But the fruit of the Spirit is love, joy, peace, patience, kindness, goodness, faithfulness, gentleness, self-control; against such things there is no law.

Mark 12:31
The second is this: 'You shall love your neighbor as yourself.' There is no other commandment greater than these.

John 16:13

When the Spirit of truth comes, he will guide you into all the truth, for he will not speak on his own authority, but whatever he hears he will speak, and he will declare to you the things that are to come.

John 4:24

God is spirit, and those who worship him must worship in spirit and truth.

Isaiah 12:5

Sing praises to the Lord, for he has done gloriously; let this be made known in all the earth.

Colossians 3:14-17

And above all these put on love, which binds everything together in perfect harmony. And let the peace of Christ rule in your hearts, to which indeed you were called in one body. And be thankful. Let the word of Christ dwell in you richly, teaching and admonishing one another in all wisdom, singing psalms and hymns and spiritual songs, with thankfulness in your hearts to God. And whatever you do, in word or deed, do everything in the name of the Lord Jesus, giving thanks to God the Father through him.

Psalm 95:1-6

Oh come, let us sing to the Lord; let us make a joyful noise to the rock of our salvation! Let us come into his presence with thanksgiving; let us make a joyful noise to him with songs of praise! For the Lord is a great God, and a great King above all gods

Galatians 6:9

And let us not grow weary of doing good, for in due season we will reap, if we do not give up.

John 4:23

But the hour is coming, and is now here, when the true worshipers will worship the Father in spirit and truth, for the Father is seeking such people to worship him.

Jeremiah 29:11

For I know the plans I have for you, declares the Lord, plans for welfare and not for evil, to give you a future and a hope.

Matthew 19:26

But Jesus looked at them and said, "With man this is impossible, but with God all things are possible."

Chapter 12 – Meeting Daniel

Romans 12:2

Do not be conformed to this world, but be transformed by the renewal of your mind, that by testing you may discern what is the will of God, what is good and acceptable and perfect.

Isaiah 40:31

But they who wait for the Lord shall renew their strength; they shall mount up with wings like eagles; they shall run and not be weary; they shall walk and not faint.

Proverbs 3:5-6

Trust in the Lord with all your heart, and do not lean on your own understanding. In all your ways acknowledge him, and he will make straight your paths.

Isaiah 30:18

Therefore the Lord waits to be gracious to you, and therefore he exalts himself to show mercy to you. For the Lord is a God of justice; blessed are all those who wait for him.

Psalm 37:34

Wait for the Lord and keep his way, and he will exalt you to inherit the land; you will look on when the wicked are cut off.

Psalm 130:5-6

I wait for the Lord, my soul waits, and in his word I hope; my soul waits for the Lord more than watchmen for the morning, more than watchmen for the morning.

Psalm 138:8

The Lord will fulfill his purpose for me; your steadfast love, O Lord, endures forever. Do not forsake the work of your hands

1 Peter 1:6

In this you rejoice, though now for a little while, if necessary, you have been grieved by various trials,

Isaiah 46:9-10

Remember the former things of old; for I am God, and there is no other; I am God, and there is none like me, declaring the end from the beginning and from ancient times things not yet done, saying, 'My counsel shall stand, and I will accomplish all my purpose,'

1 John 1:9

If we confess our sins, he is faithful and just to forgive us our sins and to cleanse us from all unrighteousness.

John 14:6

Jesus said to him, "I am the way, and the truth, and the life. No one comes to the Father except through me.

Ephesians 5:19

Addressing one another in psalms and hymns and spiritual songs, singing and making melody to the Lord with your heart,

Romans 5:8

But God shows his love for us in that while we were still sinners, Christ died for us.

Revelation 4:11

Worthy are you, our Lord and God, to receive glory and honor and power, for you created all things, and by your will they existed and were created.

Chapter 13 – The Eagles

James 3:17

But the wisdom from above is first pure, then peaceable, gentle, open to reason, full of mercy and good fruits, impartial and sincere.

Psalm 150:1-6

Praise the Lord! Praise God in his sanctuary; praise him in his mighty heavens! Praise him for his mighty deeds; praise him according to his excellent greatness!

1 Peter 5:5

Likewise, you who are younger, be subject to the elders. Clothe yourselves, all of you, with humility toward one another, for "God opposes the proud but gives grace to the humble."

Psalm 136:1-26

Give thanks to the Lord, for he is good, for his steadfast love endures forever. Give thanks to the God of gods, for his steadfast love endures forever.

Psalm 23:1-6

A Psalm of David. The Lord is my shepherd; I shall not want. He makes me lie down in green pastures. He leads me beside still waters. He restores my soul. He leads me in paths of righteousness for his name's sake.

1 John 4:18
There is no fear in love, but perfect love casts out fear. For fear has to do with punishment, and whoever fears has not been perfected in love.

Matthew 23:12
Whoever exalts himself will be humbled, and whoever humbles himself will be exalted.

1 Peter 5:6
Humble yourselves, therefore, under the mighty hand of God so that at the proper time he may exalt you

Matthew 11:29
Take my yoke upon you, and learn from me, for I am gentle and lowly in heart, and you will find rest for your souls.

Psalm 37:5
Commit your way to the Lord; trust in him, and he will act.

Proverbs 16:3
Commit your work to the Lord, and your plans will be established.

Romans 12:2
Do not be conformed to this world, but be transformed by the renewal of your mind, that by testing you may discern what is the will of God, what is good and acceptable and perfect.

John 15:7
If you abide in me, and my words abide in you, ask whatever you wish, and it will be done for you.

Matthew 7:7
Ask, and it will be given to you; seek, and you will find; knock, and it will be opened to you.

Chapter 14 – Jack, my best friend

John 15:13
Greater love has no one than this, that someone lay down his life for his friends.

Proverbs 18:24
A man of many companions may come to ruin, but there is a friend who sticks closer than a brother.

John 15:15
No longer do I call you servants, for the servant does not know what his master is doing; but I have called you friends, for all that I have heard from my Father I have made known to you.

1 Corinthians 15:33
Do not be deceived: "Bad company ruins good morals."

Ecclesiastes 4:9-10
Two are better than one, because they have a good reward for their toil. For if they fall, one will lift up his fellow. But woe to him who is alone when he falls and has not another to lift him up!

1 Peter 2:24
He himself bore our sins in his body on the tree, that we might die to sin and live to righteousness. By his wounds you have been healed.

Isaiah 53:5
But he was wounded for our transgressions; he was crushed for our iniquities; upon him was the chastisement that brought us peace, and with his stripes we are healed.

James 5:16
Therefore, confess your sins to one another and pray for one another, that you may be healed. The prayer of a righteous person has great power as it is working.

Proverbs 17:22

A joyful heart is good medicine, but a crushed spirit dries up the bones.

Philippians 4:5-6

Let your reasonableness be known to everyone. The Lord is at hand; do not be anxious about anything, but in everything by prayer and supplication with thanksgiving let your requests be made known to God.

Chapter 15 – At home with you

Isaiah 43:2

When you pass through the waters, I will be with you; and through the rivers, they shall not overwhelm you; when you walk through fire you shall not be burned, and the flame shall not consume you.

John 14:6

Jesus said to him, "I am the way, and the truth, and the life. No one comes to the Father except through me."

Luke 10:27

And he answered, "You shall love the Lord your God with all your heart and with all your soul and with all your strength and with all your mind, and your neighbor as yourself."

Philippians 1:6

And I am sure of this, that he who began a good work in you will bring it to completion at the day of Jesus Christ.

Romans 12:12

Rejoice in hope, be patient in tribulation, be constant in prayer.

Romans 15:13

May the God of hope fill you with all joy and peace in believing, so that by the power of the Holy Spirit you may abound in hope.

James 1:2-4
Count it all joy, my brothers, when you meet trials of various kinds, for you know that the testing of your faith produces steadfastness. And let steadfastness have its full effect, that you may be perfect and complete, lacking in nothing.

Matthew 5:9
Blessed are the peacemakers, for they shall be called sons of God.

Psalm 4:8
In peace I will both lie down and sleep; for you alone, O Lord, make me dwell in safety.

Chapter 16 – Dinner

1 Thessalonians 5:18
Give thanks in all circumstances; for this is the will of God in Christ Jesus for you.

Jeremiah 29:11
For I know the plans I have for you, declares the Lord, plans for welfare and not for evil, to give you a future and a hope.

James 1:5
If any of you lacks wisdom, let him ask God, who gives generously to all without reproach, and it will be given him.

Philippians 4:13
I can do all things through him who strengthens me.

John 10:27
My sheep hear my voice, and I know them, and they follow me.

John 14:16-17
And I will ask the Father, and he will give you another Helper, to be with you forever, even the Spirit of truth, whom the world cannot

receive, because it neither sees him nor knows him. You know him, for he dwells with you and will be in you.

Psalm 37:5
Commit your way to the Lord; trust in him, and he will act.

Hebrews 13:8
Jesus Christ is the same yesterday and today and forever.

John 14:6
Jesus said to him, "I am the way, and the truth, and the life. No one comes to the Father except through me.

1 Corinthians 16:14
Let all that you do be done in love.

Chapter 17 – A new home

1 Peter 2:24
He himself bore our sins in his body on the tree, that we might die to sin and live to righteousness. By his wounds you have been healed.

2 Corinthians 12:9-10
But he said to me, "My grace is sufficient for you, for my power is made perfect in weakness." Therefore I will boast all the more gladly of my weaknesses, so that the power of Christ may rest upon me. For the sake of Christ, then, I am content with weaknesses, insults, hardships, persecutions, and calamities. For when I am weak, then I am strong.

2 Corinthians 5:17
Therefore, if anyone is in Christ, he is a new creation. The old has passed away; behold, the new has come.

John 3:16
For God so loved the world that he gave his only Son, that whoever believes in him should not perish but have eternal life.

Numbers 6:25
The Lord make his face to shine upon you and be gracious to you;

Joshua 1:9
Have I not commanded you? Be strong and courageous. Do not be frightened, and do not be dismayed, for the Lord your God is with you wherever you go.

Proverbs 15:3
The light of the eyes rejoices the heart, and good news refreshes the bones.

Romans 12:12
Rejoice in hope, be patient in tribulation, be constant in prayer.

Isaiah 41:10
Fear not, for I am with you; be not dismayed, for I am your God; I will strengthen you, I will help you, I will uphold you with my righteous right hand.

Isaiah 40:31
But they who wait for the Lord shall renew their strength; they shall mount up with wings like eagles; they shall run and not be weary; they shall walk and not faint.

Exodus 15:2
The Lord is my strength and my song, and he has become my salvation; this is my God, and I will praise him, my father's God, and I will exalt him.

Chapter 18 – Friendship?

Philippians 4:6
Do not be anxious about anything, but in everything by prayer and supplication with thanksgiving let your requests be made known to God.

Philippians 4:7
And the peace of God, which surpasses all understanding, will guard your hearts and your minds in Christ Jesus.

Psalm 119:130
The unfolding of your words gives light; it imparts understanding to the simple.

Proverbs 4:7
The beginning of wisdom is this: Get wisdom, and whatever you get, get insight.

Psalm 19:7
The law of the Lord is perfect, reviving the soul; the testimony of the Lord is sure, making wise the simple;

Galatians 5:22
But the fruit of the Spirit is love, joy, peace, patience, kindness, goodness, faithfulness, gentleness and self-control.

Jeremiah 29:11
For I know the plans I have for you, declares the Lord, plans for welfare and not for evil, to give you a future and a hope.

Colossians 3:17
And whatever you do, in word or deed, do everything in the name of the Lord Jesus, giving thanks to God the Father through him.

Joshua 1:8
This Book of the Law shall not depart from your mouth, but you shall meditate on it day and night, so that you may be careful to do according to all that is written in it. For then you will make your way prosperous, and then you will have good success.

Psalm 1:2
But his delight is in the law of the Lord, and on his law he meditates day and night.

Philippians 4:8
Finally, brothers, whatever is true, whatever is honorable, whatever is just, whatever is pure, whatever is lovely, whatever is commendable, if there is any excellence, if there is anything worthy of praise, think about these things.

Psalm 19:14
Let the words of my mouth and the meditation of my heart be acceptable in your sight, O Lord, my rock and my redeemer.

Proverbs 15:22
Without counsel plans fail, but with many advisers they succeed.

John 14:6
Jesus said to him, "I am the way, and the truth, and the life. No one comes to the Father except through me."

Isaiah 43:19
Behold, I am doing a new thing; now it springs forth, do you not perceive it? I will make a way in the wilderness and rivers in the desert.

Isaiah 40:31
But they who wait for the Lord shall renew their strength; they shall mount up with wings like eagles; they shall run and not be weary; they shall walk and not faint.

Proverbs 1:5
Let the wise hear and increase in learning, and the one who understands obtain guidance,

Isaiah 30:21
And your ears shall hear a word behind you, saying, "This is the way, walk in it," when you turn to the right or when you turn to the left.

Psalm 119:105
Your word is a lamp to my feet and a light to my path.

Psalm 25:4-5
Make me to know your ways, O Lord; teach me your paths. Lead me in your truth and teach me, for you are the God of my salvation; for you I wait all the day long.

Proverbs 16:9
The heart of man plans his way, but the Lord establishes his steps.

Chapter 19 – At Jesus' feet

John 8:32
And you will know the truth, and the truth will set you free.

John 4:24
God is spirit, and those who worship him must worship in spirit and truth.

John 17:17
Sanctify them in the truth; your word is truth.

Psalm 25:5
Lead me in your truth and teach me, for you are the God of my salvation; for you I wait all the day long.

Ephesians 4:15
Rather, speaking the truth in love, we are to grow up in every way into him who is the head, into Christ,

Philippians 4:6-7
Do not be anxious about anything, but in everything by prayer and supplication with thanksgiving let your requests be made known to

God. And the peace of God, which surpasses all understanding, will guard your hearts and your minds in Christ Jesus.

1 Peter 5:7
Casting all your anxieties on him, because he cares for you.

Proverbs 16:3
Commit your work to the Lord, and your plans will be established.

Luke 1:37
For nothing will be impossible with God.

1 Corinthians 10:31
So, whether you eat or drink, or whatever you do, do all to the glory of God.

Psalm 147:3
He heals the brokenhearted and binds up their wounds.

Romans 12:2
Do not be conformed to this world, but be transformed by the renewal of your mind, that by testing you may discern what is the will of God, what is good and acceptable and perfect.

Psalm 107:20
He sent out his word and healed them, and delivered them from their destruction.

James 5:16
Therefore, confess your sins to one another and pray for one another, that you may be healed. The prayer of a righteous person has great power as it is working.

John 15:7
If you abide in me, and my words abide in you, ask whatever you wish, and it will be done for you.

Chapter 20 – The boundaries of my heart – 1

Isaiah 43:2
When you pass through the waters, I will be with you; and through the rivers, they shall not overwhelm you; when you walk through fire you shall not be burned, and the flame shall not consume you.

John 3:16
For God so loved the world that he gave his only Son, that whoever believes in him should not perish but have eternal life.

Proverbs 24:3-4
By wisdom a house is built, and by understanding it is established; by knowledge the rooms are filled with all precious and pleasant riches.

Psalm 91:1-2
He who dwells in the shelter of the Most High will abide in the shadow of the Almighty. I will say to the Lord, "My refuge and my fortress, my God, in whom I trust."

Jeremiah 29:11
For I know the plans I have for you, declares the Lord, plans for welfare and not for evil, to give you a future and a hope.

Joshua 1:9
Have I not commanded you? Be strong and courageous. Do not be frightened, and do not be dismayed, for the Lord your God is with you wherever you go.

2 Corinthians 5:17
Therefore, if anyone is in Christ, he is a new creation. The old has passed away; behold, the new has come.

Colossians 4:2
Continue steadfastly in prayer, being watchful in it with thanksgiving.

1 John 4:18

There is no fear in love, but perfect love casts out fear. For fear has to do with punishment, and whoever fears has not been perfected in love.

Isaiah 40:31

But they who wait for the Lord shall renew their strength; they shall mount up with wings like eagles; they shall run and not be weary; they shall walk and not faint.

Romans 15:13

May the God of hope fill you with all joy and peace in believing, so that by the power of the Holy Spirit you may abound in hope.

Psalm 37:4

Delight yourself in the Lord, and he will give you the desires of your heart.

Isaiah 12:5

Sing praises to the Lord, for he has done gloriously; let this be made known in all the earth.

Colossians 3:14-17

And above all these put on love, which binds everything together in perfect harmony. And let the peace of Christ rule in your hearts, to which indeed you were called in one body. And be thankful. Let the word of Christ dwell in you richly, teaching and admonishing one another in all wisdom, singing psalms and hymns and spiritual songs, with thankfulness in your hearts to God. And whatever you do, in word or deed, do everything in the name of the Lord Jesus, giving thanks to God the Father through him.

Matthew 18:20

For where two or three are gathered in my name, there am I among them.

Chapter 21 – The boundaries of my heart – 2

Proverbs 16:9
The heart of man plans his way, but the Lord establishes his steps.

Galatians 6:9
And let us not grow weary of doing good, for in due season we will reap, if we do not give up.

Isaiah 40:31
But they who wait for the Lord shall renew their strength; they shall mount up with wings like eagles; they shall run and not be weary; they shall walk and not faint.

Jeremiah 29:11
For I know the plans I have for you, declares the Lord, plans for welfare and not for evil, to give you a future and a hope.

James 3:17
But the wisdom from above is first pure, then peaceable, gentle, open to reason, full of mercy and good fruits, impartial and sincere.

Proverbs 1:7
The fear of the Lord is the beginning of knowledge; fools despise wisdom and instruction.

1 John 4:8
Anyone who does not love does not know God, because God is love.

Mark 12:29-31
Jesus answered, "The most important is, 'Hear, O Israel: The Lord our God, the Lord is one. And you shall love the Lord your God with all your heart and with all your soul and with all your mind and with all your strength.' The second is this: 'You shall love your neighbor as yourself.' There is no other commandment greater than these."

1 John 4:18
There is no fear in love, but perfect love casts out fear. For fear has to do with punishment, and whoever fears has not been perfected in love.

Ephesians 3:20
Now to him who is able to do far more abundantly than all that we ask or think, according to the power at work within us,

The Way of Love – 1 Corinthians 13

1 If I speak in the tongues of men and of angels, but have not love, I am a noisy gong or a clanging cymbal. **2** And if I have prophetic powers, and understand all mysteries and all knowledge, and if I have all faith, so as to remove mountains, but have not love, I am nothing. **3** If I give away all I have, and if I deliver up my body to be burned, but have not love, I gain nothing.

4 Love is patient and kind; love does not envy or boast; it is not arrogant **5** or rude. It does not insist on its own way; it is not irritable or resentful; **6** it does not rejoice at wrongdoing, but rejoices with the truth. **7** Love bears all things, believes all things, hopes all things, endures all things.

8 Love never ends. As for prophecies, they will pass away; as for tongues, they will cease; as for knowledge, it will pass away. **9** For we know in part and we prophesy in part, **10** but when the perfect comes, the partial will pass away. **11** When I was a child, I spoke like a child, I thought like a child, I reasoned like a child. When I became a man, I gave up childish ways. **12** For now we see in a mirror dimly, but then face to face. Now I know in part; then I shall know fully, even as I have been fully known.

13 So now faith, hope, and love abide, these three; but the greatest of these is love.

Printed in Great Britain
by Amazon

82165525R00120